FOR MICHAEL —D

HOMƎ

WITH LOVE,

MARK MACDONALD

[signature]

ARSENAL PULP PRESS
Vancouver

HOME
Copyright © 2001 by Mark Macdonald

ARSENAL PULP PRESS
  103-1014 Homer Street
  Vancouver, B.C.
  Canada v6b 2w9
  arsenalpulp.com

The publisher gratefully acknowledges the support of the Canada Council for the Arts and the British Columbia Arts Council for its publishing program, and the Government of Canada through the Book Publishing Industry Development Program for its publishing activities.

This is a work of fiction. Any resemblance of characters to persons, living or dead, is purely coincidental.

Design by Solo
Cover photograph by Mark Macdonald
Printed and bound in Canada

CANADIAN CATALOGUING IN PUBLICATION DATA:
Macdonald, Mark, 1970-
  Home

  ISBN 1-55152-110-5

1. Home-fiction. I. Title.
PS8575.D6562H65 2001   C813'.6   C2001-911280-7
PR9199.3.M31154H65 2001

HOME

FOR IRENE

Contents

A photograph of someone's mother. She is wearing white, but standing—posing—before a newly white-washed suburban house. She is ghostly in the bright sunlight. She will die by her own hand in the garage on a Sunday afternoon in summer.

A cake of morphine, broken into little pills and diluted. Someone will forget their pain from cancer with this drug, and tumble down the stairs, believing for the first time that they are Superman.

A pamphlet distributed by nurses in a war, 1955. Cleanliness and attentive care will alleviate even stubborn vermin. Twice during wartime this pamphlet was used to kindle house fires.

———•◦•———

Some new fruit: Perhaps the first revelation of a tamarind, the candy tartly tasted and the name of the fruit forgotten. Maybe a persimmon or a dragon's eye. A wormy peach, purchased naïvely from a market kiosk on a first trip abroad.

———•◦•———

A tarot card used to scoop the magician's ashes, picked at random, and placed into the wind. Floating, it will find its place in the sea. His simple gift of wisdom.

———•◦•———

Calamine lotion which painted the skin a pinky-white for a lifetime of childhood—"It seems he's prone to insect bites." It was a chalky exoskeleton relieved only by epsom salt baths.

———•◦•———

MACDONALD

An old map, refolded, that once indicated directions for a car trip, north out of town. Rescued from a glove box, the map itself smells of oranges and premoistened towelettes.

———◆•◆———

Biological artifacts: A bottled owl; a grimacing face—its cross-section pressed against the glass to reveal the sinuses; the five-legged circus calf. These items teach us, by their mere existence, a lesson some would certainly avoid, embracing ignorance.

———◆•◆———

A boatswain's whistle, brass and silver, that called to rafts a doomed crew. Its tone cannot be reproduced in shrillness.

———◆•◆———

The odour of lemon gin and some youth's first drunk. That tangy stench will forever evoke dread and its own unique place in the pantheon of haunting spirits. A beaker of puke.

———◆•◆———

Contents

A set of prisms and looking glasses, which, when correctly lit, project intricate patterns in a darkened room. The whole of the cosmos simplified in consistent, paint-by-number comic strips. In the old days, these things could be used to animate an image of a horse and rider, a martyr's flogging, and the four seasons of a mountain ash.

———•◦•———

A tiny vellum envelope containing a lock of auburn hair tied with a piece of crimson silk. This had been inserted between the pages of Job in an oversized family Bible. Passed down solemnly through generations, each time it lost more significance; each time the ancestor, to whom the hair belonged, grew more forgotten.

———•◦•———

The notes of a pornographer, his itemized list of tricks and snares. Cheap, beguiling manipulations, effective beyond their right to arouse, and instant in their nostalgia.

MACDONALD

DEATHS

From fairly early on in Dad's illness, we all knew that our involvement would be total. My sister and her husband, my mother, various cousins and neighbours, all managed to band together so that Dad was never alone. The air of mutual support was reassuring, and certainly enabled each of us to endure the slow trauma of watching his life end. Various of us would move into the house for a time, touching off another, allowing for them to get away for however long. Together we were a kind of team, in a situation that would kill a person on their own with its physical and emotional demands.

He had been terribly frail for some time, gradually losing capacity in this or that part of his body, his mind competing with the painkillers. We would sit together in the spring sun, bringing him food and pills, and he would spout profound observations that held a dying man's significance to us. He spoke about passing airplanes, the axis of the earth at this time of year, the political turmoil in the Middle East, the migration flights of obscure birds. We beheld this strange wisdom, sometimes confused by it, other times inspired. But it seemed like a performance, as though he were demonstrating that his mind was still very much alive, despite the deficiencies of his body. As difficult as it was for us to watch his increasing vulnerability, we felt that if he simply let go, he would be in a more peaceful place. None of us wished him any harm, but it was somehow becoming clear that his time was overdue.

After the first year of living together with him, we began to realize that he was really struggling to resist his approaching death. We patiently spent each new day as though it was simply additional to our experience and to his life. The situation had become so routine that we wondered exactly why he was holding on so tenaciously. Was it for our sake or his own? It seemed to be an important distinction, not so much steering the course of his eventual demise, but compelling him, feeding his private motivations, finding each new footing on whatever path he was about to take. The rest of us had more or less abandoned our own lives in aiding his, and our new way of living had become a kind of compromise between life and death.

Then one morning, as the end of summer approached, he summoned us all to his bedside. He thanked each of us in turn for the sacrifices we had made. He made a deeply moving speech about conclusions, closure, and punchlines, and then he just closed his eyes and ceased to be.

After all the long days and nights, all the emotional ups and downs, we sat together around him, each of us crying tears of relief as much as loss. None of us could deny that it had been an extremely trying time, but we had each discovered a courage and tenacity that we had never realized in ourselves. Finally it was over, and we entered a period that felt like a long, all-encompassing sigh.

Each of us was prepared for the arduous tasks of arranging the funeral and so on, and we went about our assigned errands in an automatic state, utterly drained of emotional energy. As the ambulance was pulling in to the driveway, and my sister was on the phone to the undertaker, Mother let out a terrible shriek. We all rushed to Dad's room, stunned in slack-jawed disbelief that he was alive again. He had simply sat up in his bed and flung the sheet off, blinking at us like we were a bunch of idiots.

He asked for a glass of water.

In a state of shock, I rushed to the kitchen for a clean glass. My sister rang the undertaker back, stuttering awkwardly. In an effort to make him comfortable, Mother carefully adjusted his pillows, as I tried discretely to snuff the candles that were lit around his bed. Almost ashamed, my sister gathered up the funeral shroud that he had flung to the floor. As we busied ourselves returning his room to the state it had been in, we made quick, wide-eyed glances at each other as if to check if this was

Deaths

all really happening. Indeed, he was very much alive, and after making an uneasy sort of apology, he asked for a bite to eat.

Though none of us were prepared for the shock of Dad's return, we had been ably trained over the past years to meet the needs of his care, and we soon had the household running the way it had been, with him the centre of attention. The routine returned, but with a sense of bewilderment. He had definitely died. He had been dead for several hours, and awoke with his faculties intact—even improved, as though his heart and mind had taken a much needed break.

But that was only the first time. The next time he died, some months later, none of us were as quick to act. With an uncertain hesitance, we once again covered him with the sheet. We waited until the following day before we called the undertaker, after staying with him in turns throughout the night, assuring ourselves that he was, in fact, completely dead. The undertaker, with an under-standable reluctance, even conferred with the family doctor before agreeing to load Dad into the hearse. We felt cautious as the doctor and funeral directors con-sulted and went about their tasks. We followed the hearse at a slow speed towards the funeral home in our various cars like a kind of pre-funereal procession.

Still several blocks from the funeral home, the hearse pulled over and we all knew what to expect. Against all logic, Dad had revived again, and this time he was quite cross. Who could blame him, riding along to his funeral? Once again, we felt a combination of disbelief, desperation,

MACDONALD

and relief as we returned home. Once again, we un-packed the humidifier, the bedpan, the boxes of medi-cine, and all the other accessories of homecare.

Despite his dismay at being shuffled off to the grave, Dad eventually approached his repetitive dying with a humour that eased the situation for all of us. The third time he returned from the dead, we began treating it more as a minor nuisance. We were all exhausted after taking care of him for so long, and his new program of habitual death and ressurection was an unwelcomed ad-dition to the routine of our daily chores. Emotionally drained, the stress of his illness meant little to us any-more, but his repeated deaths were trying on us in a new, unique way. We began to speculate privately on ways of keeping him dead, but no one dared interfere with his fate. Each new death seemed so final, but there was always his stubborn return.

The undertaker had stopped taking our calls.

We came to realize that the situation would persist. We discussed various ways in which to adapt to Dad's bizarre needs. My sister's husband finally made a sug-gestion we could all live with, and he recruited the help of some sympathetic co-workers. With their guidance, we drew up plans for a kind of family crypt. There would be enough room for Dad's coffin, beds for the rest of us, electricity, plumbing, a space heater, books and so on. It was more like an old-fashioned fallout shelter than a traditional mortuary, but it would meet all of our needs. Twice during the construction of the crypt Dad died and returned. Each time he awoke with a mix of

Deaths

apologetic concern and vexation that we were treating him like a corpse. By this time, all the usual associations and uncomfortable realities of death seemed like someone else's problems.

A year to the day after Dad had died for the first time, the whole family moved into the crypt. It was difficult to leave the house behind, but our tomb proved to be entirely liveable. My brother-in-law's friends had laboured long and hard on our behalf, and after a few weeks, the crypt really felt like home. I began charting Dad's cycle of life and death on an old calendar, and discovered a quite regular pattern. We were able to predict his next death and resurrection, and in time we started celebrating them like birthdays, each time with a feast, followed by drinks and dancing.

Soon life in our family crypt became so comfortable that we forgot about our past lives. None of us wanted to leave the place for any length of time, and we realized that we had become quite agoraphobic. We would send out for food and clean laundry, the anxiety of the outside world of our past too much to deal with. None of us felt comfortable outside of the grave, away from Dad's corpse, so we had the place sealed. A system of dumbwaiters was installed, and became our only contact with the world of the living.

We sometimes wonder if Dad will live forever this way, by dying over and over. Will the same fate befall each of us like some genetic predisposition? Whatever the case, we have found peace now, and the future of life in our tomb seems bright. The lesson of Dad's death has

MACDONALD

taught us to live in a whole new way, and we wonder
what more we could have asked for.

Deaths

PUSS

'm lying here in bed. I don't want to get up. Under the bandages, I sting. Puss did the sheets yesterday. He didn't have to, so to make it up to him, I imagine cooking a really nice meal, a big feast. So soft to lie here, the duvet is so soft. He flipped the mattress when he made the bed, and I can feel a roundness, a comfort. Between the mattress and the duvet, I feel like a big old sandwich. The sheets smell good too, and clean.

I was mincing in the kitchen. I was mincing garlic. I was making Puss a grand feast, ingredients leaping into place. Puss was hungry, and I love cooking so much. When I cook him something really good, and afterwards, he's full, he can enjoy looking at his things that much more, and I feel good when he feels at home. Anyway, chopping the garlic up, so fine . . . I was lost in chopping, and I cut my thumb.

The cleaver went down on each lobe of garlic. Shuck shuck shuck shuck shuck. My old thumb got in there and wham! From the tip to the part just by my old nail, it came clear off but a strand, and hung there. The garlic stung. Jammed into my mouth, sucking like a vacuum cleaner. The cold tap water hurt. I got these cute kid's band-aids, you know, with cartoon characters. I put one on but it didn't stop the blood. It was sad and funny at the same time to see the little characters turn red from behind.

———•◦•———

I can flip over and stretch alone in the bed. Puss is downstairs looking at his things. I can stretch and stretch and stretch. You know those cold corners of the bed, where your foot hasn't been in a while? It's cooling and warm at the same time. The duvet is very thick and soft.

———•◦•———

After the garlic, you know, in the dinner for Puss? I was really careful. I would use a knife, but I was scared of the cleaver. He didn't know I cut myself that time. I was careful not to get the food and blood mixed up. He was in there, looking at his things, and my thumb was stinging in the bathroom.

MACDONALD

Then I cut my hand. I am clumsy, you know? I cut my hand badly, across the back. It was deep and I saw the bones and I didn't want to tell Puss. I had to tell him because all I had were those kid's band-aids with the figures from cartoons. This time there was blood in the food. Puss came in and helped me. I stayed in the kitchen until he got the car all heated up. By the time he took me to the doctor, it didn't sting any more. I just felt like my hand was in a big cold mitt. I didn't figure I'd lose my hand. Puss is helpful a lot of the time.

———•◦•———

I drift in and out of sleep. Sometimes I lie awake, coming out of a dream, and it lasts just a minute before it disappears. The dream sort of lingers, and I wonder if it's not really happening to me. Other times I'm thinking hard on something and it makes its way into my sleep. When you can stretch out, and curl the duvet around you, you know? It's so soft.

———•◦•———

I cut my old arm off, well, at the elbow. It felt the same way as when I got garlic in my thumb. Most of all it really stung, but I remember being surprised, too. In the immediate moment after, it was like I was shaving and the razor slipped. You know? There is a moment when you realize, and then there is a moment after. I saw all the blood coming out. I saw the skin there. I felt so clumsy, and it really did sting, too.

Puss

Puss came again. Puss helped me cover up the bloody spot, but even when we were cleaning the towels, the water ran red. Cuts are like that. It's okay now, you know? The bleeding has stopped and the doctor has gone. I'm okay now. And Puss will get his food one way or another, a nice feast.

Now he's in there, looking at his things again. I love Puss.

Maybe I'm scared. I don't want to get out of bed today. Sometimes I worry about cooking for Puss. I don't want to cut myself again or take him away from his things. And those knives are all so sharp! The big cleaver has rust on it now because I haven't used it since I cut the garlic that time. I put it in a lower drawer, with the sharp blade facing a corner. The other knives are all sharp, too. I cut myself using the paring knife once. I'm so clumsy, but I really do love cooking for Puss, you know? It's good when he's full and feels at home.

———•◆•———

I don't want to get out of bed today. It's so soft. I am round in this bed, like a big cat, and I don't want to get out. Maybe Puss will cook today, and make me a nice feast. I can stay in bed as long as I like, and he'll cook for me. Puss will cook for me today, so I don't want to get out of bed. Under my bandages, it stings, but Puss will cook, you know? I don't want to get out of bed today.

MACDONALD

A Peso's Fables

In Puerto Vallarta, across the cobbled street from the big cathedral with the funny fibre-glass dome, down an alley, and behind a thick wooden door, an old lady sits, night and day, and tells fables for a peso. Manuel told Lily about her, describing her with an air of mystery, and perhaps fear. The old storyteller, like many things in Mexico, had always been there, ancient and solitary, as long as Manuel could remember anyway. She would recite fables off the top of her head for just a little bit of money, to one person at a time, and made a kind of living that way. Lily went to her once, and with some convincing, she'll tell the story.

She waited outside until the door opened, half expecting to see some local or perhaps another tourist emerge with an enlightened expression on their face, but instead found the old storyteller alone in her single, sparsely furnished room. She was instructed to sit across the table from the old woman who poured them both a sweet lime drink into little clay cups. The storyteller, whose English was not perfect, had no trouble getting the business out of the way before starting. Lily laid a peso down and the woman shifted it to the centre of the table, exactly between them. Then she began.

She told Lily of another elderly woman, this one quite well off, her husband having been a general or something, who grew very famous as a collector and cataloguer of the exotic. She lived in a huge white house on the hill above the town, and devoted every waking moment to organizing and reorganizing her vast collections. She had rooms full of coins, stuffed birds, Russian religious icons, miniature paintings, fossils, odd bones, rare plant specimens, feathers, antique books and maps, and all manner of *objets d'art*. Every single piece in each collection was described and listed in beautifully bound catalogues, which composed a library, a sort of collection of their own. She devoted her entire life to this project, and many people traveled great distances to view her collections, some actually bringing contributions and gifts to add to the displays.

She was widowed, and lived alone in her organized little world for many years. Finally, when her age and ailing health became too much a reminder of her own mortality, she began to collect and catalogue her own body. With the last of her inheritance and investments, she paid corrupt surgeons to begin what she called a disassembly of her very flesh. Her toes were the first to go,

MACDONALD

each one painstakingly preserved with bee's wax and displayed all together behind glass, mounted on red velvet. Her teeth and hair were removed and similarly mounted, then her legs, and finally her fingers, arms, and ultimately her bones and organs. She had carefully catalogued these pieces before they were disassembled, and had left strict instructions on their proper display. Her house and collections were left to the state in honour of her husband, and visitors who make the journey up the hill are still greeted at the entrance by the grand display of the collector herself, all frames, cabinets, and bottles.

The old storyteller sat back and smiled. The moral of this story, she said, was that those who endeavour to cast their own brand of order on the world shall eventually perish at their own hand. She picked up the peso and dropped it into a small woven purse.

Lily sat back and pondered this, more surprised than satisfied. She had expected a greater universal and profound moral to the story, and felt that the old collector had fully realized that she was to become part of the collection. It was an interesting story, but lacked the kind of obvious lesson that she had hoped for. Of course, Lily is first and foremost a diplomatic woman, and so she laid down another peso, figuring that at least if she heard another fable, the contrast might offer more clarity. The old lady again moved the coin to the centre of the table, poured more of the lime drink into their cups. She closed her eyes, and sat back, and after a moment, told Lily the following tale.

A Peso's Fables

His were a disorganized people. His family and ancestors, indeed his entire community, existed without set roles or even titles that one might expect. There was no sense of parents or children, of tradition or heritage. They lived on the plains and merely took what they needed from their surroundings, shearing the animals they captured when they were cold, or eating them when they were hungry. Though the plains were surrounded by farmers, hunters, herdsmen, and artisans who created great works of art and spirituality, his people lived with none of these things. They lived communally, but each member of the community provided only for themselves, and sometimes for their elderly or immature neighbours.

Their exceptional way of life became big news for certain anthropologists who arrived in little teams from far away places and asked odd questions that he felt had no answers. They asked him where he was born, who gave birth to him, what he wanted to do in life, and he knew none of these things. He rarely talked with other members of his tribe, and it was never about these riddles. He grew up happy not knowing, and really had no curiosity about them until the seed was planted in his head by the anthropologists. Slowly, he began to consider what lay ahead in life aside from eating and sleeping and once in a while having sex with the men and women of his tribe. These thoughts worried him, and he began to see in himself a need for meaning and place which he found troubling.

MACDONALD

The anthropologists left, seemingly impressed for some reason by his lack of answers, and for the first time that he could remember, he felt uneasy, somehow more alone and isolated than before, even when he knew all the people who lived with him. He talked about these new feelings with the others, but no one could relate. They were happy with what they knew, and couldn't conceive of the notion of a broader meaning to things. That was when he decided to discover an order to his experience, a meaning of life if you will.

The others eventually began to avoid him, each deciding for themselves that he was probably mad. He spent more and more time pondering life rather than living it. He would spend long hours alone in the desert, eating and drinking less, growing more isolated each day. Eventually he died, more alone, sad, and confused than he had ever imagined possible. He was forgotten by the rest of his people who went on living.

Once more the old storyteller sat back. She sipped the rest of her lime drink, and announced that the moral of this story was that those who invent a need for meaning shall perish by their own hand. This time, Lily felt even less satisfied with the ending. She wondered if all of the old woman's stories were as nihilistic and tragic. Not being one to leave without feeling she got her money's worth, Lily placed a third peso on the table. The storyteller rolled her eyes at this point, but then moved the coin to the middle of the table, poured two more cups of the lime drink, closed her eyes, and began.

A Peso's Fables

A very long time ago, when Paul the Fifth was the pope in Rome, and Spanish priests came to teach the Indians about their single, vengeful god, there was an Augustan scholar that the local people liked very much. His name was Emmanuel de Villegas, and he was an artist, too, and drew many sketches of the plants that grew in the area, which he would send back to Europe on the boats that came and went.

Villegas took particular inspiration from a flowering vine that grew all over the place, and he named it Flos Passionis. He would tell the local Indians that if they studied the way the flower was built, its basic architecture and exotic beauty would reveal to them the passion of Christ on the cross. They would look at each other in wonder, unsure what the old priest meant, but they loved him, so they learned to recite his strange lessons back to him, and they taught these to their children, still unclear on their actual meaning.

It came to be that the old Augustan's teachings about this plant were talked about in Rome. Fearing some sort of heresy, the pope sent one of his top men, a monk named Bosio, to meet with Villegas, and to witness this unusual flower first-hand. Bosio had seen the drawings of the vine, and had learned much about its structure from correspondence with Villegas. He knew that a column rose from the centre of the flower, representing the column of the flagellation of the Lord. The top of this column split into three separate pieces, symbolizing the nails used to crucify. Precisely seventy-two tiny spokes radiated from the bottom of this structure; the same number

MACDONALD

of points on the crown of thorns placed on Christ's head. Beyond these spokes were ten petals used to illustrate the disciples present at the crucifixion. The remarkable similarities went on and on, and Bosio was very anxious to see this miraculous flower.

When he finally arrived in Mexico, Villegas took him high up into the mountains to see the vine growing with abandon through the jungle, with these spectacular blossoms scattered all up and down its length. He was scandalized! The flowers were garishly coloured, and oozed nectar. Their perfume was sickly sweet. Each one was a graphically sexual organ, highly specialized to invite the probing tongues of birds and insects. The vine itself grew so copiously as to suffocate the surrounding landscape. This was no symbol of Christian purity, but rather a weed planted by the Devil himself.

Bosio left as quickly as he had arrived, and the local people watched in awe as these two priests made such a fuss over a common weed. They were confused, too, when their beloved Villegas was sent away from their town, and when the Jesuits arrived and ordered all these simple plants to be destroyed in fiery heaps. They felt sure that something very important was happening to them because of this plant, but they couldn't quite determine what that might be. Villegas was stripped of his title and expelled from the Augustan order, and died some years later by his own hand.

Lily was told that there was a moral to this story, too. That two men can view the same wonder and be inspired to rapture or to violent revulsion, and that neither

A Peso's Fables

interpretation can ever be correct. The old woman deposited the peso in her little purse, and politely hinted that Lily should leave, having heard more than her share of stories and taken up most of the afternoon. Once again, Lily felt more than a little cheated, but she agreed to go, and she thanked the old woman despite herself.

As it turned out, Lily's visit to the old storyteller kind of ruined the rest of her vacation. Not only had the fables been less revelatory than confusing, but the lime drink had given her terrible stomach cramps. To this day she is troubled by the stories and their abstract lessons, like they left her with less wisdom, rather than more. These days she tells friends who are to travel to Mexico, that if they ever happen to be in Puerto Vallarta, and hear of the old woman who tells fables for a peso, across the cobbled street from the big cathedral, that they should just keep walking past her thick, wooden door.

MACDONALD

FLIGHT

Our new pastor came to us from the prairies, some tiny church on a broad plain. He carried a small black and white photo of the church like it was his birthplace, and he spoke of it with pride. I don't think he could ever fully adapt to our little town, tucked in the valley between rolling hills. The modest church and residence he took over were situated at the end of the town, at its lowest point, tucked amongst tall maples that kept it in nearly permanant shade. However he felt about his home, he loved his congregation, and won their hearts by taking a very active role in the community.

His name was Moffat, or Pastor Moffat, and not once did I hear anyone refer to him by Emmanuel, his given name. He had always seemed like an old man to me, but I was pretty young then, and apparently the year he left us he was only thirty or so. Mom and Dad had aspirations for me in the church and they encouraged me to spend time with the Pastor. At a time when the first really public prosecutions of corrupt priests were taking place in other communities, my parents fell over themselves to ensure that I had lots of the Pastor's attention. They never considered for a moment that he couldn't be trusted on long afternoons with a schoolboy, and they were right as it turned out. I just thought it was strange, and it was the first glimpse I had of the Pastor's power in the community—maybe power over the community. It wasn't evil, but it felt like he could do whatever he wanted. It was kind of exciting.

Sunday mornings the pews were full, and after a couple of hymns and prayers, Pastor Moffat would launch into his sermon. He played the crowd well, and I would watch as the townsfolk would lean forward, their eyes widening, enraptured with his wisdom and charisma. He would get this kind of glow on his face, and his expression reflected the palpable enthusiasm in the room. He'd build the mood right up until his arms were swinging and his voice boomed, and then, perfectly timed, he'd lean back, his hands on the altar, and deliver his message. We'd all sing, and close with the Lord's Prayer. Outside, after the service, he would greet people one by one, and everyone seemed relieved and envigorated. You could hear them walking away from the service saying, "That's a damn fine preacher man," and so on.

I'd ride my bike down the river road to his squat wooden house, sandwiched between the church and the cemetery, and he'd be waiting for me, all smiles and enthusiasm. His house was great, stuffed to the rafters with all the records of the town and the surrounding countryside going back for generations. All the photos and newspaper clippings, the journals of the last four pastors; it all formed a detailed archive of every significant moment of our town's history. Pastor Moffat showed me grainy old shots of my grandparents' wedding, records of their births and the birth of my mother. Funeral photos, christening photos, the opening of the new town hall—it was all there, but stored and displayed like a trove of the town's secrets. The commentary was gossipy somehow, more opinionated than the things you could find in the library.

As much as the Pastor loved the church and his congregation, as much as he loved playing such an important role for them, his real passion was flying. When he moved into the house, he brought with him a truly stunning collection of aviation memorabilia, and everywhere on shelves, in glass cases, and hanging from the ceiling were models of antique planes. His bookcases were stuffed with esoteric accounts of historical flights, even service manuals for old propellor aircraft. Framed portraits of pioneer aviators and adventurers hung from his walls and he would recite accounts of their bravery in obsessive detail.

One afternoon, when I arrived at his door, he had just dug up a large black and white photograph of Amelia Earhart from some box in the attic, and he overflowed with delight as he introduced me to the portrait like I was

Flight

meeting his oldest and dearest friend. She looked so beautiful in her little leather flyer's cap, so full of life and spirit, with a calm and blissful smile like she knew something the world would never know. Together we took down a large antique crucifix from the front hall and replaced it with her. He stood back and gazed at her as if she were the Virgin Mary, full of adoration and love.

I don't remember him ever talking about it specifically, but I had the impression that his father had been killed flying a plane in some war. He never spoke about flying with any kind of dread, though, in fact, much the opposite. He had never actually learned how to pilot a plane, but he spoke about it in reverent tones, like leaving the earth far behind was his ultimate fantasy. He frequently jumped at the chance for work in the more remote parts of the north, volunteering for brief missions, especially eager if it meant flying out on one of those little float planes. This just furthered his fine reputation in the town, and particularly in the eyes of my parents who now demanded that I spend every available moment in his tutelage.

The Pastor built me my very first kite, and together we'd leave the valley, driving way up onto the surrounding ridges. Miles of string trailing behind, the kite would soar up into the atmosphere high above the town and everyone would know where we were. Once it was high enough, and flying under its own speed, we'd anchor it to the ground and sit back eating sandwiches, bathed in sunshine. He would speak ponderously about how birds learn to navigate at night on long migrations, and how

MACDONALD

you mustn't ever fly a plane into an anvil-shaped storm cloud, so vicious were the maelstroms within. These afternoons were bliss to me, and I would listen to his stories and dreams at length, at least twice a week, for three summers in a row.

Who can say what changed over those three years? The Pastor seemed different, the townsfolk seemed different—perhaps it was just my perspective changing as I approached adolescence. I noticed subtle changes in the way he spoke of flight. It had become more urgent to him, like he had found a new religious meaning to it all. He spoke of the importance—the necessity—for people to learn to fly with the vehemence some people have when they talk about adult literacy. When he spoke of flight his eyes were more intense and wild, like our old pastor's, but without the burning violence of the Scriptures. He spoke less and less about the Bible in his sermons, to the point that the locals began to wonder what was happening to their church. I knew that some of the adults wanted to report him or something, to have him replaced or disciplined or whatever they do to renegade pastors. The mother of my little sister's best friend had started to talk about Pastor Moffat like he was evil, instilling wild demonic ideas in the minds of children (meaning me), and she tried to get my parents to stop letting me visit him. My mom sort of reluctantly got on the bandwagon, but my dad still really liked the Pastor, so I ended up only being able to visit him on Mondays, after school.

Flight

If anything, the town's doubts only fueled the Pastor's fiery obsession with flight. Now when I would go over to his place, we would not go out kite-flying, but stay in his dark house watching old film reels about planes or reading about the private life of Wilbur Wright. These changes in his personality were disquieting for me, and I was both concerned for his position in the town and for his sanity. One time I asked him about the great flights of the Bible, about Ezekial and the ascension of Mary. He said that those stories could not be taken literally because people don't have wings, and without wings, you just can't fly. I said that maybe Mary was an angel, or maybe just carried by angels, or maybe you couldn't see God's enormous hands lifting her up into heaven. He was clearly uninterested in the speculations of my teenaged theology. Flight for him involved greasy old machinery, carefully designed for lovingly crafted old airplanes that roared with a deafening noise as they sped you high above the clouds. I don't think he even believed in heaven at that point.

And then his time came. Enough dissent had formed in the congregation that it became obvious he would have to leave us. I was crushed. I couldn't believe that we could get rid of the spiritual leader of our community just because some of us didn't want to hear what he had to say. But letters had been written and his expulsion was in the works. On the Sunday of what was to be his final service, the whole town showed up like a blood-thirsty mob, anxious to make a spectacle out of his shame. It was known that he had been ordered to vacate

MACDONALD

the little house beside the church that afternoon, and venomous joy shone in some of the faces of the packed church hall. The entire room fell silent as he approached the pulpit.

Despite the pressure and the animosity in the room, he led us all in silent prayer. Most of the people just watched him, and didn't even bow their heads. Only a handful of us sang with him the only hymn of the service, but the others did rise and stand out of respect for formality during the song. Everyone sat down quietly, not one of us knowing what to expect next. The moment hung in the air, and various people cleared their throats uncomfortably. Somewhere near the back a baby mewled.

Pastor Emmanuel Moffat appraised the crowd with a calm, accepting, almost beatific smile that I recognized immediately. He stared out at us, kind of above us, through the open doors of the chapel. Without uttering a word, without the slightest change to his expression, he rose up into the air above the altar, obscuring our view of the crucifix. He just hovered there for a moment, some feet from the floor, glowing as if lit from all sides. The congregation was stupified. I looked all around me at the blank stares, the white faces, the open mouths. Then, just as casually, the pastor floated above us, over pew after pew of stunned parishoners, and out the front doors of the church, into the sunlit air. We sat in complete and utter shock for a moment, and then, like an explosion, we stampeded out after him, pushing and shoving to get one final look at the miracle.

Flight

Pastor Moffat floated slowly up above the church, through the tops of the maple trees, higher and higher above the town, his arms outstretched more like wings than the arms of a crucified man. Up and up he went in a slow spiral. As he became less distinct, hundreds of feet above the earth, I could still make out his satisfied expression of complete calm, and knew that he was smiling both at me and with me. His black cassock became a tiny dot and then he just disappeared into the high clouds. Around me was the entire population of the town, all craning their necks in total disbelief, not one of them daring to speak.

When I got home, I found the large portrait of Amelia Earhart waiting for me beneath carefully folded brown paper. No note was enclosed or needed, really— just that calm, wise smile of hers. Now she looks down at me from above my desk, my final preparations for earning my pilot's license nearing an end. If anything her smile is broader now, and like some sort of all-seeing protector, she watches as I prepare to make my own ascension into the heavens. My parents' disappointment that I would prefer flying airplanes to entering the priesthood is tempered now, and though they never speak of Pastor Moffat, they too have succumbed to the fates which beckon me, and they are quietly proud of the flights I am about to take.

MACDONALD

The Appointment

He doesn't want to go through with this. His work says that he has to do it, has to get a thorough check-up, but he really doesn't want to see the doctor. Still, they say if he doesn't go to the doctor, and pass all kinds of tests, he won't get all the new things he wants.

He wants the car that comes with it. They're going to give him a sedan, a luxury touring car for long trips north, out of the city. They promised him more money, a better position, more authority, and that new car. He never thought in his wildest dreams that he would have this sort of opportunity knocking at his door, and it was certainly never his intent to be offered so much of the action, but they really like him, and that makes him feel good. It makes him feel good to be the one in his position, the one they're offering all this great stuff to, the one who isn't like the employees, his co-workers, who weren't picked. He can look at them and know that he is different—better—and against his judgment, that also makes him feel good.

He doesn't feel good all the time, and that's why he doesn't want to go to the doctor. Sometimes these things happen to him and he wonders what they are. He gets feelings once in a while that aren't right, and although he knows that the doctor might be able to help him, he doesn't want to cause a fuss. These doctors have important jobs and their time is scarce. They don't have the time to spend on a guy like him, especially not because he may just worry too much.

He weighs these things in his mind. He really wants that new car because he's never had one before. The role of being chosen by them is one that appeals to him, too. He would pack up his desk in the middle of the afternoon, in front of everyone, and they'd all ask each other questions like, "Why him?" and "Who does he think he is?" They'd all feel superior, because sometimes you have to, to save face, but he would be the superior one, the one who's got what it takes. None of them would get new cars.

It's not that he doesn't like doctors either. Well, that's not entirely true. He hasn't had much experience with doctors. He's never had a GP, and he's never gone for regular check-ups. He knows that there are unlucky people out there who have good reasons not to like doctors. He heard about that woman who got felt up when she was unconscious, and about the guy who got the wrong arm amputated and ended up with no arms at all.

MACDONALD

Or maybe it was his leg. Either way, he knows about lots of people who have reasons to be scared of doctors.

He thinks back, about his own experience with doctors, all the time he spent in hospitals as a kid. He remembers the hallways that always seemed more quiet than they were, and the nurses and doctors who were just people doing their jobs, and none of them could save anyone. He remembers the Vancouver General Hospital and the Lions Gate Hospital and St. Paul's. The Royal Jubilee in Victoria, and the Victoria General: all their miles of corridors and elevators and strange cafeterias. Some of them had new machines and new facilities, but they all had exactly the same grey, fluorescent lighting, and so they melted together in his mind. He had some fondness for the name of the Royal Jubilee because it sounded like a celebration, but it stuck out as the scariest hospital of them all.

Then he thinks about the Richmond Auto Mall, with all its new cars. One afternoon he sat in over sixty different cars that no one had owned yet, and they all smelled the same. He thinks about this and then he thinks that maybe hospitals are just like new cars: big, clean, expensive machines. They make you go in different directions, of course. When he went to see the cars, he thought they were all the same after a while, too, and so he noticed the way their steering wheels were covered, or whether they had cup holders that would fold out of sight. He felt that this was the best way to differentiate between them.

The Appointment

He wonders if anyone who goes to the hospital actually gets better.

His appointment is at eight in the morning, and he has a hard time falling asleep the night before. He doesn't want to go, and for a while he even thinks that maybe he could call in sick, and they wouldn't make him do it. But sick people go to the doctor, so it's important not to seem sick. Anyway, he's not going to the hospital, just to a doctor who will look him over and sign a form and he'll get a new car. The doctor probably won't even give him a very thorough physical either. He'll get to keep his pants on.

On the morning of the appointment, he wants to eat a hearty breakfast, but he only gets through one piece of toast, and he is so nervous that it goes right through him and he gets diarrhea. He remembers that when people give blood, the nurses sometimes tell them to come back after a hearty meal, as though the difference can be seen right away. Nurses can tell who is healthy and who needs a lot more food, because it's their job to look at people who aren't healthy and people who are about to die.

Even though he can't complete his breakfast, he feels fairly healthy. He knows that he isn't in good shape, and that he should get more exercise, but there is something else. There is something in him that isn't part of him, and sometimes things happen and he doesn't know what they are. He tries not to worry about what happens, but now and then he thinks about it in bed, when he's trying to go to sleep, and it makes him very nervous.

MACDONALD

It is Friday morning, and he can only look in at the waiting room. The nice woman who answers phones and files papers at the doctor's office told him to come a few minutes early, and, by mistake, he turned up too early, and he has to wait outside while she gets everything ready. He even sees the doctor come to work. He pulls up and parks a very nice new car indeed. The doctor's car is blue, and it must be twenty feet long. He wonders if the doctor ever trades in his cars when they lose that new car smell.

He tries to smile knowingly at the doctor, about the car, but the doctor just ignores him, and unlocks the door to his clinic, and then locks it again from the inside. Watching through the window, he sees the doctor go somewhere and then the receptionist comes and finally lets him in. She says that he is early, and that he'll have to wait for the doctor to get ready, so please sit over there. She motions to a set of over-stuffed leather chairs around a table full of magazines that are all old. Briefly, he picks up a *Time* magazine with a cover story about the Gulf War.

His mind races. He thinks about the different ways he can answer questions so that the doctor won't know that sometimes things happen to him that aren't good. The phrase "Keep your eyes on the prize" runs through his mind over and over as he tries to calm himself. He feels his heart beating too fast, and he notices that his hands are sweaty. He tries to imagine that he's on a game show, so close to getting that new car, with just a few minutes of formality beforehand.

The Appointment

The doctor comes in and exchanges clipboards with the woman at the front desk. They seem to have some kind of coded system of communication, probably so that patients won't know what they're up against. The doctor retreats back into some room he can't see, and the receptionist woman hands him another clipboard and asks him to fill out a few questions before he sees the doctor. He wonders why she doesn't just ask him the questions, or why the doctor doesn't do it, but looks at the questionnaire and begins to fill it out.

"Keep your eyes on the prize. Keep your eyes on the prize."

He fills in little boxes about whether he is allergic to different medicines, how old he is, and if he has recently suffered chest pains, fatigue, nausea, dizziness, shortness of breath, anxiety, loose bowels, hypertension, difficulty sustaining an erection, headaches, stomach pains, sinus trouble, sore joints, problems with sleeping, and so on. He answers no to all of them, and hands the clipboard back to the lady. She tells him it won't be much longer, and he sits back in his chair. He is a bit calmer now, but he really wants to get this over with.

Suddenly, she says that he can go in now, to see the doctor, and he wonders how she knows this. She takes him down a short corridor, and tells him to wait in an examination room with a bed covered in paper, a desk, a small sink, an old-fashioned scale, and posters on the wall that depict scenes of respiration and the inner ear. There are coloured drawings of bald men with the fronts of their throats missing, with veins and arteries showing.

MACDONALD

When she leaves, he hangs his jacket on a hook and sits on the paper-covered bed. It crinkles.

In comes the doctor. He closes the door behind him and studies the clipboard and the questionaire. As if the little, filled-in boxes aren't enough information, the doctor asks him how he has been feeling. His voice is deep and assured. The doctor is a big man, and makes him feel comfortable.

He tells the doctor that he's feeling fine, and that this is just a formality, and after it's all done with, he'll get a promotion and a new car and everything. The doctor smiles, and puts on his stethescope, telling him to breathe normally. The cup of the stethescope goes up under his shirt and is cold on his chest. He is breathing normally, but his heart is racing, and he hopes the doctor doesn't notice this. The doctor places the cup against his back and tells him to breathe deeply, then he makes an assuring "Mm-hm" sound.

The doctor looks through a device into his ear, and then shines a light in his eye, and then looks into his throat through another device. The doctor taps his knee with a rubber hammer and takes his blood pressure. Then the doctor puts all his equipment down on the desk, and looks at him, and asks: "Sometimes things happen, don't they? Things that aren't quite right? Don't they?"

"Aw, geez, I don't know what you mean."

"Once in a while you know that things aren't quite right. I can tell. You're going to have to be honest with me if you want it to go away."

The Appointment

His heart pounds, and he feels very uncomfortable. The doctor is right, but he doesn't know how the doctor knows so much. It's his job to know. He knows.

"Yeah, sometimes, I guess."

The doctor tells him to lie back on the bed, and when he does, the paper crinkles again. The doctor makes him unbutton his shirt, and then puts his stethescope to his chest, listening for something very specific. The doctor looks right into his eyes and says that this may sting, but it'll only take a second. Washing his hands at a small sink in the corner of the examination room, the doctor tells him how he's going to make it go away, how he'll just take it out.

He watches the doctor dry his hands and then come over and touch his chest again. The doctor's hands are warm, and his fingers push hard against his upper ribs. Then, with one big thrust, the doctor pushes his hands into him and concentrates as he feels around inside him for something. The doctor grabs onto somthing, and he's right—it stings. He pulls a short cord out of his chest that looks like a stubby red snake. The end of the cord is moving on its own.

The doctor puts the snaky thing in a bag and ties the bag shut, and puts it in a plastic box with a biohazard warning symbol on it. The doctor turns to him and wipes his chest with a tissue and says that that's it—he can go. It's all okay now.

He looks down to where the doctor's hands went inside him, and there isn't even a scratch. He doesn't know what the doctor did, but as he's buttoning his

46

shirt, he thinks that the doctor must be a very good one. He does feel better, too. He sort of wants to ask what the snaky red thing was, but he's sure that the doctor knows his job. The doctor is washing his hands again, rubbing blood and stuff away into the small sink.

The doctor says, "Hey, have a good time with your new car," and then he picks up the clipboard and leaves the room. The doctor is not in the foyer when he comes out and the woman at the front desk just smiles at him and tells him to have a nice day.

He doesn't know what happened in there, but he likes that doctor. Now, in his new car, a big blue one, he heads home. He's going to take it on a long drive this weekend. The appointment is over, and his week is over, and they gave him a brand new, blue car. He's going to pack some food and a thermos, and he's going to drive north, out of town. He feels pretty good, too, and he'll be back on Monday morning to receive his new assignments, but this weekend is his to enjoy. And enjoy it he will.

The Appointment

The Telling

She reclines in a wood and lambskin chair, handed down the generations like a coveted family name. In the shade of buildings, right in the street, she relaxes, her long dark hair attended by two young women who pleat and braid with expert speed. They are dressed in the reddest of their finery, tightly woven wools with silk and beads by needle. They tug and fold and massage her head, working her scalp like dough, and as much as she surrenders to this ecstasy, as much as she yearns to fully enjoy the touch, her mind is elsewhere. At her feet, another pair of maids rub and knead, and apply intricate designs to her skin in henna and turmeric. Barefoot, it seems she wears sandals of the highest quality, such is their work.

Her hair, her feet, the heat of the day, the coolness of a shadow.... The cackle of mynahs nesting and the trickling music of water over smooth stones.... She wants to rejoice, but her mind is elsewhere. As the hands caress and twist her body, as the fingers nimbly press her flesh, she is imagining a world outside her own. These are forbidden thoughts, an arena of fantasy proscribed by her ancestors, but hers alone to indulge. The Telling calls her back, and she flinches slightly. For a moment she is self-conscious beneath the probing and artful fingers of her dressers, but the Telling begins its dance in her mind and she relaxes for a whole new set of reasons.

The Telling is the telling of time. Like the world around her, it has no beginning and no end, but it relates a definite story. She must learn the words in their sacred order, each syllable, every intonation, all the subtle nuances, until she can repeat them all at will. Tomorrow she will begin her recital, and when she is finished her lifetime will be behind her. For all the spoiling preparation and ceremony of this afternoon, she knows she has a role to play beyond her own humble desires and aspirations. She is one of the sacred instruments on which the Telling is played, and her performance must be flawless.

The muscles of her neck and shoulders are kneaded under knuckles and slapped by the heels of palms. She peers up the inlaid walls that tower overhead and cast deep shadows. Jasmine and the fireworks of passion flowers wind in long and fragrant vines from a fat urn, high on a balcony above. As the words flow through her mind and the expert hands perfect her flesh, she is transported. The delicate attentions of her maids and dressers and the florid poetry of the Telling combine to envelop her in a great velvety blanket.

MACDONALD

The syllables appear in her mind, falling into place with graceful precision, each creating a need for the one to follow. A gilt and scarlet stream of characters passes before her, floating along the twists of jasmine and between the exertions of each attendant. She is floating, too, amongst the verses and harmonies, the cool touch of a breeze across her skin, the smoothness of the fingers that pleat her long hair, and with each new line she is closer to heaven.

When at last she embarks, and begins to utter the Telling, new maids will appear to massage her throat, bring sweet oils of mint and nutmeg to her lips, and ensure that she is perpetually ready to continue the verse. As the women, young and old, retreat into the shadows, a new maid approaches who applies decorations to her lips with a paste of rose and beeswax. Her mouth is the organ which will give life to the Telling, and must be handled with care and presented as the source of whatever will follow.

Her maids will bring bricks of sweet pollen to dye her legs and thighs a pale gold. The aphrodisiac qualities of this substance will ensure a fully sensuous Telling, and its hot aroma mingling with her sweat will attract insects to descend and copulate between her legs. Other, older attendants will monitor her progress, transcribing the verse as it emerges from her body in practised hands on ivory tablets. They will produce and light long, tapered candles as twilight approaches. They will wipe away the flecks of blood around her mouth as the Telling continues, and kiss whispers of encouragement in her ears when

The Telling

she pauses for the refreshment of specially blended teas.

The Telling will go on and on like this for days in most cases, and she will eventually succumb. When her body can no longer produce a single sound, when her silken voice has been utterly sacrificed to the syllables and melodies and words she must pronounce, she will be carried from that site in the arms of young girls. They will lift her from her sacred chair and wonder in silent glances to each other as she is borne to her place of final rest.

These young girls will fantasize and speculate on just what kind of woman the Teller was. What did she experience as the cruel words of the Telling issued from within? As they train and memorize and prepare themselves for the day when they too will be called on to recite their own parts of the Telling, they will try to imagine what visions, which emotions drove the words from her body. Would they come to know the same ecstasy?

Gazing towards the blue sky, she will recline in a seat specially designed for this purpose. As perfumed women of various ages anoint and decorate her entire body, she will once again see the words and characters, each nuance of the Telling, as they wind in gilt and scarlet letters along the fragrant, twisting vines of jasmine that issue from a fat urn, high on a balcony above.

MACDONALD

WALLS

s the car sped past fields and acreages, tiny cottages, and large country manors, I visualized what I might expect when I reached the crest of that last hill, when Ian's fantastic mansion and grounds came into view.

When he found out he was sick he went through a natural phase of depression and cynicism. His family was understandably concerned, the whole concept of his illness being new to them. One of his aunts, a wealthy old spinster, too old and frail to care for her ancestral home, offered him the job as a kind of grand project that would at least provide him with distraction. He was given the care of the old house and the land it crowned, as well as a substantial sum of money to restore the now decrepit place to its original splendour.

That was well over a year ago, and at the time I was choked with envy. The project presented innumerable challenges, but filled me with decadent visions of a lit fire in every large room, knotted gardens winding around the grounds, livestock nibbling on manicured lawns. Polished wood paneling, and the family's collection of fine artworks hung proudly amongst gleaming marble and gilt ornamentation. We would need whole new outfits to wear here when it was all done.

Ian had received the news of his inheritance with idle calm, almost as though he knew it was coming, but he did not. The magnitude of the project did not sink in until he and I first pulled up the winding driveway in front of the house. Tall grasses overran the various fountains and ponds and hedges that had grown wild for a generation. The house itself, though magnificent in its architecture, had been enveloped in wanton ivies and creepers. Two chimneys had partly collapsed and various cornices and gargoyles had cracked or fallen to the gravel in front of the lavish Georgian entranceway.

I stopped the car and we stood in awe of the place. From the front of the house, on its little hill, we could see the surrounding property, the creek that ran between small lakes, the orchard that had gone unchecked and wild. Beyond that, neighbouring farms could be seen, separated by stone fences or thin lines of poplars.

He inserted his comically large key into the front door, and as it opened, stale, pre-owned air spilled out. We entered like schoolboys convinced the place was haunted. Our hearts raced.

I spent the first two days with him, prying shutters and windows open, filling the space with fresh air and light, and exorcising the thick blanket of dust that clung to every horizontal surface. We explored the many rooms, the miles of corridors, and the grand attic that ran the length of the house and allowed access to the roof in various places. We found a substantial collection of furniture and art, and began to set up his living quarters, the centre from which he would expand a liveable empire into the rest of the building. By the time I left him, he seemed genuinely pleased with his prospects. He would have to hire a team of helpers and gardeners and artisans, and I think he regained a sense of the future that had been robbed from him by his illness.

I returned to my own life like returning from a dream vacation. The city moved too quickly and my familiarity with its quirks and inhabitants left me with a sense of emptiness. This feeling rapidly dissolved into the job, the friends, the routines that I was used to, and enjoyed after all. Ian and his country castle seemed to exist in another world altogether, and time rapidly filled the distance between my first visit and the next. A year passed. I had heard nothing from Ian for such a long time that I decided another visit was due.

Visions of peacocks patrolling lawns around topiary shrubs and newly dredged and restocked fish ponds danced in my mind. The mansion would gleam from its perch on the hill, and inspire passers-by with a sense of the majesty of bygone eras. An army of determined workers would continue to clip, polish, paint and otherwise improve the place. Jealously sought invitations to lavish parties here would cause otherwise polite citizens

Walls

to come to blows. As the car sped to the crest of a neighbouring hill and brought the house and its driveway into view, I realized these fantasies were not to be.

I slowed the car to a crawl up the winding gravel lane toward the house. Clearly, the lawns had been mowed and the hedges clipped. The blanket of ivy had been stripped from the house, but the orchard had been left untouched, and the waterways remained clogged with reeds. The grey stone of the house did not gleam, and the only evidence of structural improvement were previously ruined chimneys. These had been rebuilt in brick and surrounded by a lattice-work scaffold of timbers. The whole place seemed rather less magnificent than the first time we had seen it.

I assumed Ian or one of his staff would hear the approach of my car, but no one appeared to greet me. No one came when I knocked on the giant oak-panelled doors. These were unlocked, so I pushed forward into the grand foyer of the house, and my heart sank at what lay inside.

Three very large bundles of two-by-four lumber crowded the front hallway. A table saw and various other tools lay partially buried in an ocean of sawdust. Buckets and barrels and heaped sacks of plaster mix became visible as I entered further. I called his name and it echoed down the corridors. Silence. Then came the distant but distinct sound of someone hammering a nail. I closed the front doors behind me and ventured into the house, straining to determine the source of the sound— the kitchen possibly, or one of the upstairs bedrooms?

MACDONALD

Much more furniture had been distributed through the hallways and rooms, but all of it remained covered by protective sheets. Little stacks of paintings lay on the floor, against the walls, but these, too, were covered. No evidence of new paint or wallpaper could been seen, but many cracks and holes in the walls had been repaired by plasterwork that formed an unsettling, crisscrossed web of stark white lines down the corridors. More disturbing were the elaborate frames and braces, all constructed from precisely cut two-by-fours that could be found along nearly every point where the walls met the ceiling. This strange lattice-work had also been applied to most of the doorways, some to such an elaborate effect that movement from one room to the next was restricted, and I had to move sideways into the large kitchen.

Ian looked up at me from his work. "Hey!" he chirped. "I didn't hear you come in."

"Yeah," I said. "I had to follow the sound of your hammer. . . . So, how's it coming along?"

"Good, good. . . . It's slow, but man, you wouldn't believe how much there is to do."

He was unshaven and filthy, but his physical health appeared to be all right. He seemed cheery enough, more enthusiastic than I remembered seeing him ever before, but it now sank in for me that even faced with the enormous scope of the repairs needed to the house, he had obviously not consulted with any carpenters or other experts. As we spoke, he continued to hammer away at a new construction so that we had to raise our voices to be heard. He was building some sort of framing structure

Walls

around the drains and pipes beneath the luxuriously large sinks. Dozens of intricately cut pieces of wood had been nailed in place to form a kind of unnecessary support for the hanging weight of the plumbing, and many more of these oddly shaped blocks surrounded him on the floor.

I asked if I could help and he shook his head. He encouraged me to go and get comfortable. There were beer and sandwiches to be found in the icebox, he said, and it would only be a few minutes before he could join me. Looking around, there was no obvious place where I could "get comfortable," so I overturned a couple of crates for seats and placed a third between them as a makeshift table. I fetched two bottles of beer and some apparently store-bought sandwiches from the cooler.

Admittedly, I was relieved to see him in such a perky mood. The many signs that pointed to complete insanity on his part seemed less important now, perhaps just a different way of achieving the same goal. He joined me, and smiled proudly as he chewed his sandwich. "What do you think?" he asked.

I told him as strategically as possible that I was surprised at how slow the work was going, "But it's good to see the outside cleaned up. . . ." He revealed to me that the yard work had been the only labour he had hired out. Apparently some conflict of priorities had developed between him and his gardener, and after the crucial work had been done, the gardener had been dismissed.

MACDONALD

"At least he got the vines off the outside of the house," he said. This seemed to have been the "crucial work" that the gardener had disagreed about. Even to my untrained mind, tending to the fields and waterways, the many flower beds, even the rose arbour that had nearly vanished from sight beneath the unchecked plant life would have taken priority long before freeing the house from its tangle of ivy.

"So what's with all the two-by-fours?" I asked, gesturing toward the jigsaw of wood, nails, and screws he had been working on.

"Well, you've got to do the groundwork first. Can't really procede with decorating until the structure is stable. There was a storm up here a couple of months ago. You should have heard this place creak! I went up to the attic, and you could actually feel the place rocking in the wind." He swayed back and forth and made creaking sounds to illustrate his point, and I was reminded of seasickness. I could not imagine even a hurricane shifting the structure of this building. It sat like a titanic stone on its hilltop, utterly implacable to the elements. Perhaps a draught through the aged walls and windows, but not the rocking of a ship in a swell. . . .

He went on and described the way the house sounds at night, settling into its ancient foundations, the floors and walls creaking under its own weight. He told me that he had discovered a family of raccoons in one part of the attic, and how one night, when they went out foraging on the grounds, he boarded up their entrance and removed their soiled nest. He revealed that early on,

Walls

he had arranged with one of the local boys to fill his order for groceries once or twice a month, and that even his clothes, medications, and building supplies had been delivered. I wondered if he had actually ventured outside in recent memory, but decided not to ask. I also chose not to press him about the need for the wooden infrastructure he was obsessively building in the house or about the state of his personal hygeine. It was becoming abundantly clear that Ian was suffering from some sort of advanced cabin fever, and there was something vaguely sinister about the development of his compulsions.

After lunch, he returned to his work on the kitchen draining system and insisted that there was nothing I could possibly do to help. I decided to go into the local town for supplies, and told him that I would at least prepare a dinner for us. He seemed indifferent about this prospect, and slightly more distracted by the work at hand, so I departed.

By the time I returned, dusk was approaching, and I could hear the whine of the table saw from outside. He stopped the saw when I came through, a look of genuine surprise on his face. "Oh! You're back!"

I left him to his careful prep-work. He was slowly filling a box with variously sized and angled bits of wood for the next stage in some further construction somewhere in the house and he seemed quite absorbed by the task. I went to the kitchen with my bags of supplies, again wondering about the point of the structure around its main entrance that necessitated squeezing through and then reaching back to carry in one bag at a time.

MACDONALD

I soon realized that the gas had still not been hooked up to any of the stoves, but found a small, two-element hotplate and decided to make do. I enjoy cooking, and could not fathom the need for a hotplate in the midst of a kitchen that could accommodate a staff of ten preparing a feast for sixty. Regardless, I began to prepare a soup and marinate some locally caught trout. To my horror, I discovered that the kitchen taps had to be run for several minutes before the brown tinge from rust and disuse would leave. Determined, I waited for clean water to flow. A bit of salad and some fresh bread, and we would have a decent meal, even if we had to eat it without the luxury of a table or chairs.

I had also bought Ian a new razor, some soaps, and even a toothbrush. I brought these to him, back at the table saw, and encouraged him to set his work aside for a bit and get washed up. At this, he almost seemed to take offence, but I insisted, and he eventually conceded that he might benefit from a bath. He strode off toward his living quarters and returned an hour later, not dressed for dinner, but wearing a new set of blue coveralls that still showed the press-marks from having been freshly withdrawn from their packaging.

These details of his strange new personality produced in me a resolve to make him relax for just one evening. I would use force if I needed to, but for now I just poured him a glass of wine. He followed me back into the kitchen from which the aroma of the soup was issuing. We sat uncomfortably on our overturned crates and I told him about my trip to town. He responded to

Walls

my details about the surprising range of amenities offered there with "Really?" and "Oh," and "I had no idea." Evidently he had not even ventured down the road in the last year. I wondered how he had contacted his grocery boy and the briefly employed gardener.

I was gratified when he appeared comforted by a flavourful and freshly-cooked meal. He opened a second bottle of wine as I tidied up the dishes and stored the ludicrous little hotplate in its cupboard. As we sipped our wine, darkness fell outside, and the whole house grew cold with surprising speed. I produced a bottle of quite fine single malt that I had brought from the city, and suggested we take it in front of a fire. Again he seemed unprepared to entertain in this casual way, but invited me up to his small suite in the middle of the house where he said there was a fireplace and even a radio. The liquor was loosening him up, and I felt at ease with him for the first time.

As the night wore on, and the whisky came out, he grew more animated. He seemed happy—or free, I think. I began to accept his peculiar lifestyle, half deciding that it was informed by his illness as much as anything. But I also grew bolder in my examination of his world. Why, precisely, was he so compelled to strengthen and reinforce the walls of such an immovable stone building?

Through the heat of the scotch, he explained: "Too often we take for granted the structure of things. We live in a world so artificially constructed and the denial of our mistrust in the stability of things is our only survival mechanism. Imagine being in an elevator when the cable snaps! Down you plunge. How far will you fall?

"Imagine the earthquake, the mudslide, the tidal wave. Whole towns asleep and cozy in one instant, in the next it's buried beneath twenty feet of earth and concrete. Just like that. A woman goes shopping in a department store and falls through the stairs of the escalator, into the grinding mechanism below. The airplane, damaged by nothing but overuse, simply shuts down and falls from the sky."

He moved closer to me with a very serious expression. "You lie in bed at night, and the only sounds you can hear are the building around you moving and shifting under the strain of gravity. Somewhere inside yourself you hear the same process going on, the buckling and snapping. . . . Cells collapsing, organs slowly shutting down. This is the sound of your own viscera congealing into lumps, the lumps breaking down, metasticizing, spreading the contagion further into you. What do you do to strengthen your inner structure?"

He glared at me, expecting an answer. It was all sinking in. Somehow he had turned himself inside-out. He had become a kind of immune system for the whole house, attacking each indication of entropy as he came across it. The ghosts that haunted this strange old mansion originated in the deepest regions of his own physiology. I suddenly felt ill.

I imagined Ian racing about this giant mansion, desperate to patch a fissure in the wall or a creaky stair before the entire structure collapsed to rubble around and

Walls

on top of him. He clearly sensed my unease, and likely felt he had revealed something like a terrible secret. Abruptly, he suggested we retire, and I was relieved. This revelation of his was something I would need time to digest, and I felt woozy from the drink.

I awoke with the splitting headache I deserved, but Ian was nowhere to be seen. From somewhere far off in the house, perhaps the attic, came the sound of hammering. Tap-tap-tap-pause. Tap-tap-pause. Awkwardly, I gathered my things and loaded my car. I felt as though his confession had been our parting—that there was nothing left to say. I left a note on the table saw in the grand foyer, thanking him for his strange hospitality, and promising to visit again soon. I knew that I would not.

The drive back to the city was urgent. As much as I was escaping Ian's uniquely unstable world, I longed to blindly trust the elevator in my apartment building, shock-proof electrical cords, and the walls that bore the weight of the upper stories of the office tower where I worked. My need to rediscover a life without the mistrust of structural integrity was pressing. I knew that I could only endure the city if I could learn again how to live in it without thinking.

Ian would survive, too, as long as there were cracks to be filled and rafters to be supported. One day, though, his old family mansion would offer no more potential for repair. In a tangled web of braces and cross-beams, when he had finally filled the whole interior volume of his house with crutches and struts, his inner world would at last crumble and disintegrate around him. The last of his

MACDONALD

body's cells would pop and liquefy, and he would finally find peace in his fortified world.

Walls

CRYING OUTSIDE

ate. Beyond twilight. Sitting at the table by the window. It's late. It's almost four-thirty in the morning and I'm sitting at the table by the open window listening to the sleeping city. From outside there is a low hum, a combination of sounds, each one nearly inaudible in its subtlety. Waves wash up on the beach two blocks away. Single cars, cabs mostly, dominate main streets. There is no wind.

The pipes in the building gurgle slightly, then stop. The cat sleeps soundly on the couch. The wall clock in the kitchen ticks quietly. From here I can see five other apartment buildings and none of them have a single lit window. The city is asleep and for a second I get the image of walking free on a deserted planet.

The refrigerator turns on and at first it's an apocalyptic din. So is the familiar clink of my Zippo as I light another cigarette. The chair creaks as I shift back in it, and I am aware of the sound of blowing the smoke out of my lungs. A car passes nearby. Each sound blends into a bland silence, and I stare at the paper in front of me, the whiteness of it lit by the reflected and subdued glow from streetlamps eight stories below. It is faintly possible that the paper is partially lit by starlight, but the concept doesn't really work in the city.

Crying. Did I hear it? Listening. . . . I strain to hear it again. I thought I heard, just for a moment, the sound of someone crying. It was just one note, like a memory of having heard it, somewhere distant. I don't breathe, listening. I stub out the cigarette as the refrigerator shuts off. The heater burps slightly, and then the silence, as total as it can be here, once again occupies the space of my apartment. I must have imagined the sound.

Did I hear it? I quiet myself and my environment as much as possible . . . cigarette out, chair settled. . . . Some part of my soul glued itself to that sound, even if it wasn't someone crying. I lean forward, open the window a little more.

Someone is coughing, across the street or just down the block. It sounds like he is sitting up and coughing in the middle of the night. It is clearly and distinctly the sound from a different source. I sit up now, and try to lean out the window to hear it. In this silence I can isolate five different sources. One is traffic on a distant street. Two is the sound of cars passing on the street I can see. Three is the sound of the waves—and lapping waves, too. Four is the ambient sound of my apartment; the clock, the cat, the creaking. Five is the sound that I

MACDONALD

am listening for, more of a silence than a sound. Having written only the numbers one to five on my pad, I turn it over and push it away.

And then again: the sudden intake of breath, I heard it! I heard the sound again and in my dark apartment I'm genuinely pleased that someone is crying. It was that sort of gasp of someone in deep despair, a person gathering strength to continue their solitary dirge. I think it is a woman, but I can't tell. I lean out into the air around the building, but I can't get any closer to the source of the crying.

The night air is cool and for a moment it occurs to me: what if someone is watching me, from a darker apartment, leaning out into the night like an idiot, straining to hear the suffering of another one of us? A friend of mine died from leaning too far over a balcony, and the image comes to me in perfect detail, so I sit back down in the creaky chair with the simple satisfaction of having confirmed my suspicion that yes, someone is crying.

Silence.

Another note. High-pitched. It is the note found at the end of the inhalation of someone crying. That just-for-an-instant break in the octave of despair. Someone inhaling a gust of new air, new hope, more fuel for the fire. I'm happier now in the dark, in my apartment, with the knowledge that I didn't dream the misery of a stranger.

Scenarios to explain the crying run through my mind: someone upset about a departed lover, terrible news from abroad, the death of a good person, sheer

Crying Outside

loneliness. . . . The crying person is still not necessarily male or female in my mind. The tiny gusts of sobbing breath that I have heard could issue from either throat, but I suspect it is a woman. I think she is two floors below, possibly one or two apartments over from mine, and sitting farther away from her window, such is the muffled nature of her sounds. If it were not for the silence of the night time, her sobbing would have lost all of its vague clarity, and become indistinguishable.

Words are spoken. Possibly, it was the person crying —the woman—uttering something to herself that would renew her tears. I imagine her saying, "The bastard!" But it was not clear enough to hear, and once again I lean out the window, hoping she will continue. A gentle breeze has come up for a moment, and carries the sounds farther from me. They are sounds of anguish, and as the wind dies down, they once again caress my ears in the darkness.

Clearer now, they could be coming from a young man. One prolonged, quiet moan. Yes, a young man in a distant apartment, possibly across the street, privately suffering from some emotional strain or debt or yearning. He was told today that he is positive, that he will get sick. His lover has left him. His mother died yesterday morning in a faraway town he called home, and to which he cannot return. Perhaps he is simply collapsing under the burden of expectations, of unseen finances, or just the weight of the world on his new adult shoulders.

It is definitely a woman. That last gasp settled it. She is twenty-four years old and tonight, after her boyfriend

MACDONALD

told her he couldn't possibly see her because he is having an affair (she thinks), she miscarried a baby he knows nothing about. The boyfriend is callous and stupid. She alone had to face the unthinkable in her tiny apartment bathroom. She feels unwell, and fears for her own health. In the morning she will call her mother and confess the entire horrible story.

I catch myself.

Stubbing out the second last of my remaining cigarettes, I whisper something about bed to the cat. The cat stirs. I stand and drink a glass of water in my own apartment bathroom, imagining the tiles stained with blood. I look at the mirror, at the heavy bags beneath my eyes. It is enough not to know. It is too much not to care, but it is enough not to know. I will retire now, lying in bed alone, trying not to think in the darkness of my room, about the woman or man. I will try not to think about tomorrow, and about all the other people asleep and silent in my world.

Crying Outside

THE GARDEN OF
EARTHLY DELIGHTS

ay collected orchids. "Actually," she would tell me, hers was a collection of "Chinese Cymbidiums and assorted skirted Oncidiums." Orchids were her primary reason for being alive, with the Christian Science teachings of Mary Baker Eddy perhaps ranking second. Every waking moment of her day that was not spent misting, feeding, photographing, painting, and generally fussing over her large collection of orchids was consumed with re-reading the many tracts and booklets that the Christian Scientists supplied her with. Kay's life was good. It was rewarding without being demanding, and her two passions were easily funded by her savings and her late husband's estate.

I first met Kay the afternoon I applied to board with her in the large brownstone house on 45th Street. I think she liked me right away because once the formalities of introduction were over, she gave me the grand tour of her home, from the book-lined walls of the lower studies and living areas to her impressive rooftop hothouse. There was to be no phone call: I could move in at my convenience.

I was delighted, too. Kay seemed quite reserved, not the sort of person whose daily existence would interfere with mine. The house was spectacular. From the street it had a very refined look, an impression enhanced when one entered and saw the dark wood paneling and rich, luxurious carpets. Her husband had been something of a traveller, and I came to understand that he had first sparked her interest in the orchids. His tasteful collections of multicultural knick-knacks were scattered throughout the place, on tables, shelves, and on the walls. The walls were also home to many of the small, botanically accurate oil paintings Kay had made of her plants, and these were numerous and impressive in their level of skill. Soon after I moved in I discovered the special pleasure of relaxing in one of the libraries or studies, casually looking through some rare, first edition monograph on Chinese imperial families or a book detailing the discovery and botanical classification of a rare epiphytic orchid.

The greenhouse on the roof was Kay's domain, but she would show it off with obsessive enthusiasm. Here were over three hundred species of orchids, each named and grouped together, sometimes in a bewildering sort of way that would make perfect sense to an aficionado. Delicate lavender and vermilion blooms hung in long sprays in the impossibly hot and humid air, issuing scents of lilac, mint, jasmine, and citrus. Tiny fans circulated the air in the hothouse with absolutely no cooling effect. It was not a comprehensive collection of orchids, but the space was filled and Kay's ability to go through all the trouble of finding new specimens was somewhat reduced by her age. Still, she would grow wonderfully excited over a newly blooming plant, and hop up and down like a schoolgirl, pointing and sniffing, and saying, "*Oncidium macranthum*! It's Colombian! Isn't it spectacular? Smell it, darling!" Then she'd grab my head and force it towards the plant's most succulent and private parts. The plant's tiny, golden-yellow flowers with their discrete ruffles and markings were indeed attractive, but I was never transported into the heights of ecstasy that Kay's obsession found.

I helped with the shopping and with the housework. I built a new stand for the greenhouse. I drove Kay to various appointments, and helped her frame and hang her fine little paintings. Over the course of the first six months that I lived in her house her confidence in me grew, and I would be sent out on banking errands, and to pick up various prescriptions. I imagine she was in her early eighties when I met her, but, as she would say, "I'm a tough old bird!" She was one of those people who fought off frailty by sheer force of willpower, and her physical presence, her refined demeanour, education, and charisma combined into a formidable persona. We quickly grew to like each other very much.

The Garden of Earthly Delights

One afternoon, while reading about the adventures of the botanist, Sir Joseph Banks, my reverie was broken when Kay charged into the room with a look of manic enthusiasm. "Mark," she said, "we have a field trip!" She handed me one piece of the stack of mail she had been examining. It was a three-leaf, fold-out pamphlet advertising a kind of travelling floral exhibition that was due to come to town in two days. The presentation of the pamphlet was rather odd, almost Victorian in its formalized bravado. It said, "Colonel Gorse's Garden of Earthly Delights Traveling Show: Wonders of the Exotic Plant World Revealed!" The lettering was straight from some antique carnival, and the whole message was held aloft on banners, clutched at one end by a plump cherub, and at the other by a grinning devil figure. The conservative zeal of the pamphlet, and even the name of "Colonel Gorse" seemed preposterous, and right away I envisioned the Colonel as some sort of shyster who took elderly matrons like Kay for all they were worth. Yet the style and the notion of the thing appealed greatly to her, so I agreed to take her for an afternoon, and to "be amazed by ten floral wonders of the far east," even though it made me roll my eyes.

Kay's affection for her orchids was affecting me, too, and from time to time I would actually ask her for yet another tour of the greenhouse. Gradually, I was being recruited into the ranks of the plant-fancying eccentrics that she knew in such numbers and jealously admired for their collections. I began to notice the subtly different orange hues of the various hybrids in the *Oncidium* clan.

MACDONALD

Her little treasure-trove of plants was indeed spectacular. Her blooms could entrance you somehow, lift your spirits to a place of heavenly beauty, and at the same time reveal the most prurient mix of seduction and harlotry. The thought of a presentation of exotic plants, that was in itself exotic, amused me.

I had been to a number of floral shows with Kay, one or two orchid-specific exhibits, and the annual home and garden sort of thing, where retailers could showcase their new, tasteless garden sculptures and fifty new types of herbal tea that all made one's tongue recoil. There were standards to these shows and spectacles. The people they attracted were much the same, the goods offered for sale were uniformly overpriced, and often the most innovative new garden tools or hybrid plants were snubbed or disregarded by the crowds for not fitting into their set traditions. From the start, there was something different about Gorse's show.

Instead of being held in a convention centre, botanical garden, or even a school gymnasium, the Garden of Earthly Delights was housed in a large, circus-like tent, just to one side of a major freeway off-ramp. The access road, by which we could enter the smallish parking lot beside the tent, proved very difficult to find. As we circled the site for the third time, speeding down the ramp that could only lead to the main highway, I wondered aloud to Kay about how Gorse even managed to get a permit from the city to hold his little plant circus in such a bizarre spot. She supposed that maybe he only wanted to attract a certain calibre of person, and this difficulty

The Garden of Earthly Delights

we were having in finding the entrance was a kind of test. Perhaps the lower classes would give up in frustration and drive away. . . . I told her that I thought this was unlikely, but I could offer no better explanation.

We circled around and around, looking down at the odd tent and its various, large placards that tempted passersby to "Let Col. Gorse Amaze and Thrill Your Senses!" Eventually we discovered that at the very bottom of the spiralling ramp, there was an access driveway that forced us to suddenly change lanes and perform a hairpin left turn at a very dangerous speed. Although the narrow lane was unmarked, it did prove to give access to the parking lot beside the huge white tent. Not surprisingly, ours was the only car in the lot, and as we stepped out, we noticed more signs and placards informing us that we would "Never Be the Same Again" after witnessing the "Astonishing and Exotic" plant specimens within. My disbelief was now tempered with a strangely urgent curiosity to get this all over with and see what possible madness lay inside the tent.

When I first saw Colonel Gorse and a man I assumed to be his assistant standing expectantly in the tent's entrance-way, I stifled my amusement by coughing loudly into my fist. Kay was enthralled. True to form, Gorse was a very tall, impossibly gaunt man, I would say in his mid-forties. His limbs were slightly too long-looking, and his immaculate black suit and top hat brought to mind a stick insect as drawn by Edward Gorey. Everything about him, from his pointed goatee and bushy black eyebrows to his perfectly groomed outfit, seemed like an overly cultivated caricature of an evil Victorian industrialist, one who would happily run down orphans in a cobbled street to save time between visits to his factories and sweatshops. As we approached, he and the assistant simultaneously removed their tall black hats, and I muttered to myself, "Oh, come on!"

Gorse bowed like a gentleman and, with a charming smile, introduced himself to Kay, who was clearly impressed. She took his hand and introduced me as her driver, after which I was treated with a kind of polite disdain. I whispered to Kay that I would remain outside and "Tend to the horses," but with a discrete jerk of her head, I was gestured inside—she wasn't about to be astonished and amazed on her own.

The Colonel led us into the carefully controlled atmosphere of the tent, which was crowded—stuffed— with the exotic foliage of large jungle plants in ceramic urns. Vines dangled from above, and tropical birds in impressive gilt cages squawked and preened. Several tables were visible, each with its own display of floral oddities, and accompanied by the same boisterous signage. All of these tables divided aisles which converged on yet another, smaller tent, tall but plain, within the centre of the larger space of the canopy. I supposed that this inner tent housed the main feature of the show because it was set back from the other displays, separated in true carnival style.

We were led through the steamy haze of the place, from table to table, between curious blooms and enormous orchid specimens, all under the din of the screeching birds.

The Garden of Earthly Delights

Each table held its own, painstakingly organized portable bed, labeled with handwritten legends that described the plants in question and their collection by Col. Gorse, himself: "The Welwitschia emerges from the scorching soils of the Namib Desert, bearing a single pair of leaves that may survive for fifteen hundred years. During the collection of the specimen you see before you, four servants succumbed to the extreme elements of the expedition, and perished of exhaustion, dehydration, and the fits."

I stared at the sign in disbelief, wondering what "the fits" were, and speculating on Gorse's cruel treatment of his servants to recover such an ugly, diminutive plant. Clearly he carried his Victorian demeanour into his theory of plant collection. Sure enough, the plant was made up of a withered and leathery pair of leaves that curled about themselves, and surrounded a sort of spike that held aloft two grey-green organs shaped like pine cones. Again, I wondered why anyone would desire this plant for a collection. Had this plant's place in Gorse's melodramatic flower show been worth the sacrifice of four lives, or was the description of human suffering only an added fiction, tacked on for effect?

A different table displayed various types of flesh-eating plants, each one apparently designed by a madman, with bizarre shapes, grasping tentacles, and traps that snapped shut around their insect prey. Beside this, a display of African desert plants pollinated by flies, with foul-smelling flowers, the exact texture and colour of rotting meat. The next table was dedicated to toxic

MACDONALD

plants: monkshood, hemlock, devil's club, and deadly nightshade. . . .

The tables and potted plants and bird cages were set up in a kind of spiral that would ultimately lead to the smaller tent in the centre of the larger one. After witnessing Gorse's collection of exotic and cruel plant specimens on the tables that surrounded it, I was curious, despite myself, to conclude with the "grand finale." Kay was obviously growing impatient to reach the end of the tour as well, after nearly an hour in the sweltering heat of the place. I was also growing a bit disquieted that, over the course of all this time, no other vegetation thrill-seekers had appeared, and that the Colonel was lavishing so much attention on Kay.

Finally I asked when we would be able to see the famed Garden of Earthly Delights. After an hour of build-up, I expected to be astounded at least once. My question was poorly received and it was the assistant who spoke. "That particular display is not open at this time. Perhaps if the lady were to return tomorrow?"

With that, Kay and I both made for the exit. It was preposterous! Though we had paid no entrance fee, there was a distinct feeling of having been ripped off. Colonel Gorse hurried along behind us, assuring us that the Garden of Earthly Delights would certainly be worth a return visit once it was fully prepared. He said that it would be like nothing we had ever seen, and that he could promise that simply viewing the Garden would change us forever. . . .

The Garden of Earthly Delights

Not listening to Gorse, Kay muttered angrily about the gall of making an elderly woman spend such a long time in such an unpleasant atmosphere. Without actually apologizing to her, Gorse continued to follow along behind us, seeming concerned that he had caused an offence. At the front door of the tent, he stopped Kay, and took her hand, saying, very sincerely, "Please, m'lady. If you will return tomorrow, I promise you will not be disappointed."

Kay gave him one last glare, and said, "We'll see." We left Gorse and his assistant in the doorway and made for the car. The air outside seemed icy cold after leaving the tent, but it was refreshing, like waking up after a strange dream.

Over dinner that night, we exchanged very few words about the Colonel and his weird exhibits. The whole experience had been very odd, and there was something about the fact that we were both so disappointed at not seeing the highlight of the show—not the disappointment itself, but the fact that we felt that way, that was disturbing. We agreed that it was like realizing that we had been seduced. Perhaps Gorse the Showman and his ridiculous signage had truly affected us. Ultimately, we also agreed that, despite his quirky attire, and despite the lack of other patrons, Gorse did show us a grand collection of truly exotic plants. The afternoon had been worth it just to meet the eccentric Colonel himself.

Kay found me trying to study the next day. "I want to go back," she said.

"So do I."

MACDONALD

We drove the same route, took the same offramp, and made the same, life-threatening turn. Once again, the parking lot was deserted. With determination, we approached the tent, and it was Gorse's assistant who met us in the doorway. Kay said, "Please tell Colonel Gorse that we will see his main exhibit now."

"The Colonel is not here today," was the reply. "But I will happily take you to the display." Kay and I glanced at each other—of course the Colonel was absent. He had tricked us into coming the first time, and he had tricked us into coming back. His absence was a kind of subliminal punchline, but we remained intent to at least take in the Garden of Earthly Delights, so we followed the assistant inside.

The tables, plants, and birdcages had been rearranged in such a way that created an avenue between the entrance of the larger and smaller, interior tent. The effect was slightly intimidating, and I felt uneasy, like we were about to mount a very scary rollercoaster. Apparently Kay felt it, too, and took my hand as we were led forward.

Outside the curtained entrance of the small tent, the assistant stopped us. I expected a typical carny speech about being changed for life, but he proved slightly less flamboyant than the Colonel. He told us that what lay inside represented a lifetime's achievement for Colonel Gorse, and that he had spared no cost or concern in its construction. He told us that few people had ever been privileged enough to witness the Garden of Earthly Delights firsthand, and that he would be able to supply us with a glass of water afterward, but that the Colonel

The Garden of Earthly Delights

Gorse Travelling Company could not be held responsible, if, for instance, the lady should faint from shock.

Like excited schoolkids, Kay and I entered the tent as the assistant waited outside. The air inside was cooler for some reason, and the lighting was quite dim. On a long table in front of us sat a large, elaborately decorated wooden box with two small windows set in the top. The exterior of the box was extremely ornate, the entire surface covered with brass and ivory inlaid in a variety of plant motifs: vines, flowers, trees bearing fruit. . . . We could have been looking at a coffin, or a pipe organ, or at a writing desk from imperial Russia, and unlike the displays in the rest of the show, there were no explanatory signs to assist the viewer. Kay approached the thing first, and peered inside the first small window.

For a moment she was silent, like her eyes were adjusting to the diminished light within. When she turned to look at me, her face was ashen. "It's impossible," she whispered, and returned to her viewing window. I joined her at the second little glass panel and also had to squint for a few seconds, not because of the dark interior, but so that I could comprehend what lay inside.

At first the scene appeared to be some kind of tiny, perfect diorama, depicting a tropical jungle scene. In unfathomable detail, trees were visible, encrusted with vines and lianas, and forming a canopy, blocking my view of what appeared to be an acutal, real sky. The illusion was complete, and the interior space of the box seemed to extend forever in each direction. Tiny birds became visible in the trees, and they were animated

MACDONALD

somehow. The hairs on the back of my neck stood absolutely upright. This was no clockwork trickery. We were peering into an actual tropical forest, and the sudden horror of the experience shot through me.

The plants themselves undulated obscenely, the tips of their branches and tendrils grasping and strangling everything they touched. An orgiastic sense of disordered depravity, of perverse, uncontrolled growth, and of articulated evil, became apparent. The bird calls were now audible, but as cries of pain and misery that echoed through the hateful foliage. Limbs asphyxiated in the powerful clutches of twisting and savage lianas, and turned black, falling from the treetops and rotting in soft heaps on the forest floor. Snakes devoured birds and each other, until they grew swollen and burst, and armies of voracious insects swept over their carcasses. The whole mass of vegetal life consumed itself in an unspeakable cannibal feast.

Everything in the forest was evolving and growing and fornicating as if at high speed. Fruits fattened on vines and branches, and dropped to the fetid forest floor, sinking into the filth of the abomination of it all. Seedlings sprouted forth like rude worms, and scrambled up every vertical surface, blocking out the light to the less fortunate plants beneath, which withered, blackened, and died.

It was then that I saw Gorse. Clearly, distinctly, he appeared for an instant, dwarfed by the chaotic vegetation, grinning demonically at us, and biting back the various tendrils that threatened to choke him. His top hat was

The Garden of Earthly Delights

absent, and his hair was wild, but it was certainly the Colonel, or perhaps the devil himself, darting in and out of the insane disorder of plant growth. The last image I saw was Gorse yanking an engorged snake from a tree by its tail, and lunging at its throat with his white teeth.

I tore my eyes away from the scene and grabbed the hand of Kay, whose face was still pressed against the tiny glass, her mouth hanging open in shock and revulsion. She turned to look at me and again, she whispered, "It's impossible."

We burst through the curtained door, into the heat of the outer tent, and knocked Gorse's assistant to the floor as we hurried to leave the place. He called after us, asking tauntingly, "What did you think? Did you like it? Did he impress?!"

Kay physically pulled me out the door and into the natural sunlight of the real world, and neither of us spoke or looked back as we got in the car and sped out of the parking lot, onto the highway. Flabbergasted, and in a state of complete shock, we drove home, parked the car, and went inside in one sweeping motion. I poured Kay a glass of sherry, and whisky for myself, and we sat in her kitchen, alternately staring at each other in disbelief.

Of course, our visit to Colonel Gorse's Garden of Earthly Delights Traveling Show was some time ago. Kay no longer reads the works of Mary Baker Eddy, but she maintains her interest in orchids. If anything, she has imposed more order on the collection in her greenhouse, numbering each of their little pots and containers according to some botanical catalogue system.

MACDONALD

Perhaps our view into Gorse's vegetal hell brought us closer, as I can't foresee a time when I would move away from Kay. She will keep painting the tiny and intricate flowers of her orchids, and I will continue to frame them and find space on the walls of her house to hang each one. We have more time to do this now, because we no longer pay regular visits to plant shows of any kind.

The Garden of Earthly Delights

QUALITY TIME

She dreams of earlier days, when her dreams meant less, or when they seemed to mean something specific. She calls this period in her life childhood, and she feels almost certain that her memories are fond ones. From time to time she worries that she had invented many of these happy memories, filling in the blanks in a childhood she suspects was more bleak. But on a good day, she feels like a proper adult, thinking fondly back to a simpler way of living.

"Daddy, I dreamed about the carnival." Horses, tents, balloons. . . .

Somewhere along the way her life had left this innocence behind. She thinks that she has been helped to forget about that time by her disapproving family, by the complexities of trying to behave like an adult, and by the speculations of her psychiatrist and social worker. In those days she still knew how to love unconditionally, how to trust people, and how to function according to other people's rules. She had a job once, but now couldn't even recall what she did, why she did it, or with whom. She still owns a small beater car, but she is forbidden to use it, should the dreams of her adulthood suddenly take over. It is blue, except for some rust spots, and it sits derelict in front of her building as a constant reminder. She has lost not just the ability to participate with the rest of humanity, but the right.

She is resting on the edge of a titanic yellow flower, peering into its depths, trying to see the petals on the other side, but it is too wide. The blossom stretches to the horizon below a sky of the purest blue, and though she is alone here, she has no fear. Inhaling the fragrance of this other world, she plunges down the unfathomably long slide into the middle of the flower, splashing into an ocean of sunlit, golden pollen. A huge plume of it shoots into the air like a geyser of aromatic dust. It's warm here, like a hot bath, and the smells and colours surround her with a snug feeling of safety and joy.

Far away, the sound of bees.

The psychiatrist wants answers. He expects her to indulge his witchcraft and swallow the daily fist of pills, to write down these "phantasms and visions" as he calls them. He wants to convince her of the dangers of this new reality that is slowly taking over her life, allowing tiny moments of pleasure. He tells her it is a false security, and gives her a notepad to jot down her thoughts whenever she feels she is "slipping." Back at home she

MACDONALD

hides the pills in the drawer beneath the oven, and page by page, turns her notepad into a series of blue-lined paper cranes of various sizes.

She awakens from a deep slumber with her new legs cramped in her tiny room. Her knees press uncomfortably against the ceiling and her hips have widened and stretched with a pain she associates with childbirth. The inconvenience of the situation strikes her, rather than a sense of panic; how can she leave the house with these enormous legs? Her arms are too short to scratch her itchy feet. She can't fit through her bedroom doorway. She lies back, relaxing, knowing that her friends will bring her food and drink.

"I think I'll stay in today anyway, it's wet outside."

How did her legs become so overgrown? She wonders why it was only her legs that grew, and realizes how glad she is that it wasn't her breasts or her head. She thinks this is quite funny, actually, and, despite herself, she gets the giggles.

"What the hell am I going to do now? They'll call me Big Legs!"

The giggles become louder and the whole apartment begins to shake with her laughter. The more it shakes, the funnier it seems to her. She feigns disappointment and says, "I'll never ride a bicycle again!"

Her social worker arrives without food. Instead, she brings her ubiquitous, bloody clipboard.

"How was your week?" she asks.

"Aside from my legs?"

"What's wrong with your legs? Do they hurt?"

Quality Time

When she looks down, she sees that they are their regular size again. Typical of the social worker to contradict her. She raises a foot up and scratches it with her comb.

"They were bigger this morning, so I stayed in."

"Have you taken your meds?"

"...Yes." She thinks of the name "Big Legs," and stifles her giggling.

"Well, you look fine, a bit pale. You should go out this afternoon. Do you want to come for a coffee with me? My treat."

"I'm still tired. Let me sleep on it."

She turns in bed and feels the warmth of her partner, the indentation on the bed full of soft, smooth flesh and deep breathing. *Mmmmm.* Her partner turns and snuggles against her, breasts and thighs pressing warmly into her back. She smells her hair and reaches behind, draping her lover's arm over her shoulder, hand cupping breast, nipple between soft fingers. She can't recall a safer feeling, or as much love in the cozy heat of the bed. Later she gets up first and brews some tea in two cups. They sit up in bed and sip the hot liquid, listening to the rain storming against the windows, the wind whistling through the drafty attic. Once in a while, they turn and just look into each other's eyes, no words come to mind or seem necessary in the grey morning light. She passes a hand through her lover's hair and inhales the perfume of her skin.

The shrink arrives and immediately her pleasure escapes like fog down into the floorboards, between the cracks.

MACDONALD

"Were you dreaming again?" he asks. Clinical asshole.

"No."

"Any dreams last night?" He takes out a pad and slides his glasses down on his nose. It occurs to her that this is simply for affect.

"The pills seem to be helping," she says. "You were right."

He looks at her speculatively, as though she were lying, the prick.

"Oh yes," she continues, "I'm thinking of going out job-hunting again."

"That's probably a good idea. Do you want to talk some more about your father?"

She is halfway up a steep mountainside that is planted with tea. She looks down the steep slope and sees tea plants growing in tidy rows all the way down into the forest below. Uphill, the rows of plants extend right into the mist around the peak of the mountain. She is Asian for some reason and carries a very lightweight wicker basket. With tiny scissors she traces the contours of each plant, snipping. Leaves and new shoots fall into the basket, and it fills with expert speed. The air all around her is thick with the aroma of tea, and cool on her skin.

Her father comes into the room abruptly and shoots her a look of total contempt. "Still getting your head shrunk, eh?"

He turns to the psychiatrist. "You shouldn't bother with her. . . . Bit of a lost cause, this one. Her sister got the working brain."

Quality Time

"I don't have a sister and you know it," she spits back.

The doctor sits up. "I didn't mention your sister. I said father."

"Well, then I guess I don't want to talk about him."

Hours after the shrink leaves, she goes out to buy some food at the Chinese grocery next door to her building. Back in her kitchen, she heats the soup and looks for a pan for the Pillsbury-something instant cheese bread. She stares at all the pills in the roasting pan, enough to tranquilize a hippo. She chooses four based on colour alone, pulls off the capsule tops, and sprinkles the mysterious powders into the soup, adding some dried rosemary and black pepper for good measure. "And remember," she warbles in her best Julia Child voice, "you're the only one in the kitchen! Ha ha ha!"

Her soup is half finished, but she's feeling drowsy, slow, as if she were underwater. Something in the bowl, now cool on the coffee table, stirs the surface and tries to rise up. She sits back in her chair, eyes widening as the head of a beautiful serpent appears, thick like a boa or anaconda, tongue flickering like black lightning. It rises up, higher and higher, weaving its cold reptile head back and forth, perhaps looking at her, or just the room. More of the snake pours out of the bowl, its bulk coming to rest on the floor. It slithers and twists around the legs of the table and heads for safety and darkness beneath the sofa. Now its tail finally pulls from the bowl, something like twenty feet later, and follows beneath the furniture. She realizes that her feet are off the floor, her chin resting

MACDONALD

between her knees. Tentatively she steps up and toward the door, half expecting the serpent to follow her, hunt her, strangle her. But there is nothing.

In the kitchen she phones her social worker. "Can you come over?"

The social worker comes in and seems surprised by her smile.

"Please. . . . Sit, and I'll bring in some tea."

The social worker sits on the sofa, and asks from the living room, "You seem really good today, are you eating more? Have you been out at all?"

She pretends not to hear. "I'll be there in a second," she shouts over the boiling water's rumble.

As the kettle's whistle starts its slow rise in pitch, a noise comes from the living room, a suffocated yelp. The sound of glass breaking, the table toppling over with force. The boiling water is poured into the pot, steaming peppermint into the kitchen. She returns to the living room with only one cup and the teapot. She puts them on the floor and puts the table back on its legs. She pulls it over to her comfy chair, and pours a cup of greenish tea. The social worker is gone, and the tiny narrow end of a snake's tail is disappearing beneath the couch.

She feels a bit better today, becoming convinced that the multi-coloured capsules in the oven drawer might be helping her after all. She decides that maybe her shrink should come by for tea. She can thank him for all his concern and wise prescriptive care. He can sit on the sofa, and she'll bring some tea in from the kitchen. After he's gone, maybe she'll go away for a

Quality Time

while, take a holiday from the stress of her life, take a break from her hectic schedule, from the memories of her father. Spend some quality time.

MACDONALD

A Space
Called Love

He was missing, but his friends were not concerned. No one asked where he had last been seen, and no one organized a wake or sent out a search party. His absence merely replaced his presence in their midst. They missed his stories, and they missed his strange fortune-telling, but the man himself had simply turned into dust.

For many years his stories had held them in a kind of trance. Little meaningless vignettes that told them something wise about the world. No one genuinely believed that he was psychic—it wasn't like that. When he told a fortune, as he called it, he somehow just opened their eyes to a part of the world they had never considered, or offered them a dreamy view into his own. The effect was often startling.

"Two boys, one seven, the other nine, are sitting near a hammock in a yard on a suburban street. They are playing a game in the shade on a hot summer day. The younger one has a red metal robot, and he speaks for it in a high, mechanical voice. The older boy speaks through a Barbie doll that he has dressed in oversized combat fatigues that belong on one of his brother's action figures. On the doll's face he has drawn a comical handlebar moustache with an indelible black felt marker. In their scenario, the doll and the robot have met and fallen in love. Behind them, on the dry lawn, the action figure lies naked, facing down. For some reason there is shit on the figure's foot and leg."

He had lived in a world of diagnoses, watching his family and friends fall prey one by one to the realities of cancer, AIDS, madness. . . . Since his youth, every day had been spent waiting for some terminal news, but he was not depressed by this. He had found some sort of peace in his resignation, and quietly, humbly, he just waited. His world view disturbed many of his friends, but they were captivated by his tranquility and they each found ways of living around him as though he existed in a bubble at the centre of their lives.

"In a subway station in Montreal, an elderly woman, wearing all black, is waiting for her train. In her mind, she is going over the list of items she has bought that afternoon, and imagining the soup she will make. She is cleaning the vegetables, slicing them, heating chicken stock. The ingredients blend so well in her mind that she can smell and taste the result. While she is imagining her soup, her eyes are following the pattern of tiles along the edge of the track where her train will come. The brown and beige tiles are arranged in a most hypnotic way, and as she follows their lines she thinks of pearl barley and how it reminds her of Pearl Bailey. Her reverie is broken when she realizes that on the platform in front of her there is a finger. Without hesitation she stoops and picks it up, examining it closely. She thinks it belonged to a man, as there is hair in the parts between the knuckles. It is an index finger, and the nail has been trimmed recently. She thinks the cut is very clean where it was severed from some man's hand, and as she thinks this, she wraps it in a tissue and tucks it into her purse. Her train arrives."

His friends speculated that his life-long anticipation of death provided an insightful form of meditation for him, that he received visions through this meditation, and that by recounting his visions, he was paying the world back. Others truly believed that he was able to tell fortunes, but that they arrived in his mind from some distant place, that they were the fortunes of people he would never meet. Perhaps he had received these visions in error, and recounted them to keep his mind focused on his ongoing project of fate.

Whatever the truth was, his stories were his components. They came together to make up the man that they knew, and when he disappeared, all that was missing were the stories. His physical presence had become non-existent for them. His absence was a kind of completion or closure to his being. Finally, he had ceased to be, and doing this brought him in line with their perception of him.

"A man is cutting fish on a wharf on the coast of an

A Space Called Love

island in northern Japan. He has been cutting fish for hours, and he has a lot of fish left to cut. Most of the time, the man tries not to think about what he is doing because he loves the fish. He loves them as creatures of the sea, and he thinks it is unfair that so many should have to die like this. He also knows that their flesh will feed his family and many others, and that the bones and viscera they cannot use will make his crops strong and healthy. In this way he knows that the whole fish is useful, and that he is merely an agent, helping the fish to become something else. This is what he tells himself, but now and then he loses his composure. He sees the fish struggling in their pails and baskets. He watches their desperate gills gulp for air. He smells their entrails and he must pause to scrape their torn scales from his hands and arms. The suffering, the stench, the daunting task at hand makes him sick, and he turns away, vomiting over the side of the wharf. With a clean, blue cloth he wipes his mouth and dries the tears from his eyes, and he can see his vomit, diffused in the water, spreading out into the ocean, and being eaten by a frenzy of tiny fish."

His friends heard these stories—their very own fortunes, he would say—and took them as abstract lessons. They felt that he was incredibly wise to be able to tell these stories, but even impressed by his wisdom, none of them dared to join him in his bleak world view. They were casually aware of his obsession with his approaching demise, but their own lives could not afford to be lived this way. There was no room in their banal, day-to-day realities for his perception, so it was as though they

MACDONALD

merely crowded around him as he stared intently ahead, fully expecting to see an end to his journey.

Once he was gone, and though their fortunes had stopped being told, his stories hung in the air around them. His friends lived in a world whose edges were illuminated by having listened to him. The stories haunted them in a way that was free of fear or dread. The strange words that he had issued and his physical absence culminated in perhaps a greater presence than he had ever been. They could not explain this, so they called it love.

"I am walking down a path that is framed by a very long avenue of poplar trees, between a network of muddy ponds and canals. The air is cold and damp, and the sky is perfectly grey. Songbirds dart across the path, between hidden branches of the trees, and I only catch glimpses of them before they dissapear, but I can hear them chattering in the brush and high overhead. I am compelled to climb down the steep bank to the edge of one of the cold, opaque canals, and various pairs of mallards are disturbed and launch themselves into the water, paddling away from me with their rubbery orange feet. At the edge of the icy water I can see the vegetation dipping into it, the ends of leaves and reeds curling into the water. That is where I will go. Under the curling vegetation that hides the actual edge of the pond, I will slide and curl myself. Into the water, and up, under the vegetation, that is where I will go. It is cold there and the water rots the leaves into rich soil. In this murky world, hidden from above, I will reach my destination and my wait will be at an end."

A Space Called Love

HOME

There is a road that leads due north out of town. Beyond the city limits, beyond the suburbs, it heads north with an architectural intent, a straight vertical line on the maps. One or two communities are found just east, or just west of the road before it heads into farming country.

After another couple of hours' driving, it begins to cut through deep scrub and then thick forest. The road becomes the only reminder of civilization for the next four or five hours, until, once again, it cuts through little towns and villages, and then up to the inlets and islands of the far north. Supply trucks and the odd military vehicle mostly use this road, as there are no other lures for tourists and daytrippers. No campgrounds, no parkland, no resort destinations.

Donald remembered the trips his mother would take him on, heading north, up this lonely road. He remembered the preparations they would make, the sandwiches packed, a cooler full of fruit and drinks in small cartons. Clear, picture-perfect memories—and fond ones, too—of heading north with Mom. He remembered the word games she taught him: Twenty Questions, Who Am I, and the one about the last letter of a place name being the first letter of the next. He remembered eating at the truck stop in one of the little communities an hour or two out of town, and how they served gigantic breakfasts that he couldn't imagine anyone eating. Bert & Irma's it was called, but he and his mother called it Ernie & Bert's and laughed conspiratorially.

He hadn't been on one of those road trips with her for many years, and he had to think about the year that she died to place their last trip in chronological memory. He must have been eight or nine.

Donald remembered the return trips, too. How they would play a special game of Impatience with the traffic while on their way back into town. Once, she surprised him with her bawdy sense of humour when the two of them made the drivers in front of them pull off to take a pee break by sheer force of will. "You have to go to the bathroom. You have to go to the bathroom," they would chant, and it always seemed to work. The driver of the car ahead of them would pull off at a rest stop or gas station, and the two of them would burst out laughing as they drove on.

He learned to be a patient passenger this way, utterly at home in the right-hand seat, just gazing out the window at the passing landscape, the trees, the farms,

MACDONALD

the road signs. From time to time, wildlife. He knew that
they must have taken that road many times, but he was
disturbed that he retained no memory of their destination. He would think back, try to remember. . . . It's not
easy to recall the details of twenty-odd years ago. He
could remember other trips, even ones that he took with
his father and brother, when they were all together as a
big dumb family. He had seen photographs of some of
these trips—he in a plastic wash basin, bathing on a pic-
nic table, naked and fat and splashing and content. The
stories about their Siamese cat, Coco, who seemed to
love the journeys if only for the nighttime hunting. In the
morning they would wake up to eight or nine lizards,
snakes, voles, and birds, lined up on the hood of the station wagon, their heads all pointing in the same direction, tails in the other. Coco would do a special dance,
and purr loud enough to raise the dead.

The fact that he could not remember the specifics of
his trips with his mother left him melancholy, sad that
he remembered so little of the time she was alive. So
much had happened since then, and now he went about
the world as his own man, but he always felt these holes
in his memory left him incomplete somehow. There
were no grainy old super-8 movies to watch, and not a
person in the world who would know if he asked them.
He knew in his heart, though, what was coming. He
knew he would have to make the trip again if he were
ever to feel settled with himself, with his mother.

As Donald made the arrangements for his own journey north out of town, his mind raced with images of his

Home

mother, and of their car trips. His mother had been a ballet instructor, a passion and lifestyle she sacrificed for the marriage that would not last. She worried about her weight, about being out of shape, and he could never understand—she was just Mom, after all. As he booked time off work, as he shopped for his first portable icebox and the food to sustain him, detached details of the time he shared with her appeared and disappeared in his mind, and once they were gone, he could no longer recall them.

He remembered the sign on the side of the road. He couldn't place where on the journey they would pass it, but he remembered them passing it a number of times. It was a sort of billboard, alone and out of place in an isolated section of forest. Yes, it was toward the top of a small hill, and he remembered being able to see it as they came out of some trees, just sitting there, advertising to no one from across a shallow valley. He searched his mind for further details—had he dreamed it? What did it say? What message was erected in the wilderness, and to what audience was it intended?

"Love," it would say, or, "Ending." That was it. In great big cryptic letters it bore a strange word or truncated phrase on its left side, and the right depicted the same unchanging diagram, or maybe a map. His mother would turn and say, "Oh, there's the sign. What does it say this time?" They would pass it at considerable speed, but always comment, suggest their ideas at what possible meanings it held, and for whom it was intended. Donald seemed to recall that his mother wrote it off as

MACDONALD

some intentionally vague code for members of a cult or obscure church movement. Like those "Eckankar" and "Abortion Hurts Infants" billboards they used to pass sometimes on the way to the ferry terminal.

Donald continued packing, wondereding why his memory of those road trips was so jumpy and inconsistent. Was it just the years since playing all those games? Why would his memory of such a remarkable landmark come suddenly to mind? He packed his sleeping bag and his camera, and watered the plants well before climbing into his little Honda and setting off. He dropped his extra set of keys through a friend's mail-slot on the way to the highway that would take him around town and towards the exit that led north. He stopped for fuel in one of the small hamlets just past the suburbs north of town, and felt good about being so mature, making this important journey on his own. He felt like this departure was the first genuine step he had made into full adulthood.

He had forgotten how narrow the two-lane highway seemed. Occasionally there would be room for faster traffic to pass, a third lane cut into the bush at the road's edge, but there was never any faster traffic—or other cars, for that matter. The landscape was clearly used for farming, and was subdivided into attractive sections and fields, but there were no buildings or barns visible. Once in a while a pasture of cows or sheep reassured him that he had not driven into complete desolation, and from time to time he crossed a small bridge or crested a hill that seemed familiar through all those years.

Home

Nearly two hours past the last town he had seen, the landscape began to change. Low bushes and scrub now dotted the fields instead of farm animals. Isolated willow trees, poplars, the ubiquitous pine, began to appear more randomly in the brush, apparently not used as intentional property markings as before. These became more frequent and congested, and soon he had entered the forest proper. The road wound around bends so that all he could really see were trees and little tufts of wildflowers occasionally appearing in brilliant oases of colour. Here, the road was shaded from the summer sun, and the coolness was refreshing. He was thinking about where to take his first pit-stop and didn't really notice as the quiet music from his radio was replaced by static. He wished his mother were alive to offer some guidance— "Oh, there's a lovely spot just another couple of miles ahead where we should eat lunch. . . . There's a creek!"

Rounding a new bend in the road the sign appeared ahead and it might have been a circus tent, it was so out of place. Across a little dip in the road, just like he remembered, stood a full-size billboard to his right. Even from a distance he could plainly read the single word, "Soon," in huge red lettering, a kind of friendly script, almost handwritten. He grew aware that his jaw was hanging open. Nothing in his memories from childhood could do justice to the inappropriateness of the placement of this sign. Donald had not passed a single car for at least two hours, and felt comfortable slowing to an eventual standstill in his lane, ten or so yards in front of the billboard. He switched off the ignition and climbed out.

MACDONALD

The strangeness of the whole thing was monumental. To the right of the word "Soon" was an odd diagram or pictograph formed by a vertical black line that bent slightly to the left at the top of the board. Beside this and criss-crossing it in places was a broad numeral three on its side, or perhaps a curvy 'w.' It looked vaguely like a crude drawing of a bum. Above the centre point of the 'w' was a smaller circle, and above that, a curved line that pointed toward the right-hand edge of the billboard. Two more circles and a couple of additional lines and curves completed the meaninglessness of the advertisement. Dumbfounded and strangely uncomfortable, Donald reached inside the car for his camera and shot the sign from various angles, even stepping through the tall grasses that lined the edge of the road.

Somehow he felt that the sign held a kind of significance for him, but this was lost in the bowels of his memory. The ambiguity of the message was plainly disturbing, but he couldn't tell why. He looked one way and then the other, up the road. There was no traffic. Wind through the trees and a distant, barking crow were the only sounds. As he got back into the car, he had that strange tingling need to leave this spot, like a child who can't climb the stairs from a darkened basement fast enough. He looked for a spot to turn the car around, but the ditches to either side of the road made it too narrow, so he drove on, past the sign.

Some forty yards past the billboard was the entrance to a dirt road off to his right, possibly a driveway, and he slowed the car as he pulled in, fully intending to back out

Home

and head south in a single movement. A narrow thicket of trees separated the road from a wider, more open clearing, and he decided to turn the car fully around in there. With gravel crunching beneath the tires, he saw that the clearing opened onto a property with a small workyard, a garage, and a simple house at the far end. Strewn about everywhere were rusty car parts, buckets of rainwater, piles of wood, most of them overgrown with grasses and blackberries. He felt like an intruder here, and turned the car around, pausing to take one final look at the house. He froze. In the window of the rundown, blue-painted bungalow, he saw the face of a middle-aged man, handsome, but additionally spooky in this setting. The man just watched him as the car turned toward the road, smiling in a casual way, a little nod, with no sense of anger or concern about tresspassers.

Donald was totally unnerved and sprayed gravel as the car pulled back onto the road, heading south. He felt like he had just woken from a dream, like the man in the little house had been watching him sleep for a very long-time, with his disquieting calm smile. Donald floored the gas and sped past the sign, resisting a new sensation that things were falling into place for him. He had not expected to see anyone at all on his journey and, zooming back into the shadows of the forest road, he realized that part of him hoped that it would all remain a mystery for the rest of his life. A confusing childhood memory that would keep a part of his mother alive, if only in his mind.

Speeding through the trees, and still only five or six miles from the billboard and its hidden driveway, Donald's

MACDONALD

mind became still. His anxiety was slowly relieved and as the static coming from his car radio sputtered into identifiable noises and segments of music and chatter, he was without concern. In this grey state he slowed his speed and smiled to himself. He had made a great step forward, and though his journey was not yet complete, he knew he had done all the right things. It was all falling naturally into place, not only in his picture of the past, but in his guesses of what the future might bring. As he passed the scrub, the pasture land full of animals, the gas stations, and Ernie & Bert's, he knew that he understood the diagrams on the billboard, even if their meanings were still unformed. He knew that the sign had been placed there for his exclusive benefit, and had probably waited many years for his journey to read it with new eyes.

Back in town, his apartment seemed empty despite its clutter. Things he had attached importance to were pushed aside as he packed the few boxes he would take with him. He was examining his own world from a new perspective, and felt none of the usual nostalgia for a particular item of clothing or dog-eared book. Only the essentials went into the boxes. He called two people, to say goodbye, and intended to call more, but didn't in the end. He watched his old life, falling away as it was, and at times felt concerned that he was letting so much go, but after all, he knew where he was going.

The man who he had seen in the little window of the rundown bungalow was waiting for him in the driveway the following day and helped him unload the car. "Welcome home," he said to Donald, smiling, as the car

Home

was emptied. Indeed, it felt like a homecoming, and Donald knew now that all his needs would be met here. He loved this man, or a part of him did anyway, some deep part of him tucked away in his spine, in his bloodstream. An explanation of the diagram on the billboard was no longer necessary for Donald as the two of them entered the front door of the house.

Together, they whitewashed the huge sign, layer after layer, until all its details were obscured. Drivers would whiz by the empty sign, on their way back to Something Inlet or Whatsit Harbour, far further in the wild north. The two of them would be happy here in their shared household. Donald and the older man would sometimes make love, or Donald would anyway. Like the bee making love to the flower, the man's responses felt mechanical at best. Still, they both had what they wanted, and enjoyed each other.

Years later, the older man died. Donald buried him with care and held a little ceremony behind the garage, in a spot littered with generations of graves. Donald found himself emerging from another stage of life, but with greater ease this time. He was in control now, an adult. Once in a while he would repaint the rundown bungalow and make minor repairs to the property. Once in a while he would change the word on the new version of the billboard down the road from the end of his driveway. Once in a while he would stare out the window of the small blue house, waiting. He knew that eventually, in time, the front end of a new car would appear tentatively in the driveway, and for the first time, he would see a younger man peer in disbelief and half-misunderstanding at the rundown bungalow, at the face in the window. The young man would leave, but as sure as time, he would return, and Donald would welcome him home.

Home

Mark Macdonald has worked in nearly every dimension of the publishing industry, from agent to bookseller to book buyer. His stories have appeared in numerous anthologies, including *Quickies 2*, *Bar Stories*, and *Carnal Nation*. His first novel, *Flat*, was published by Arsenal Pulp Press in 2000.

He lives in Vancouver.